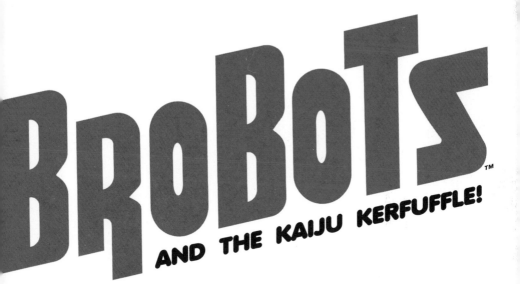

BROBOTS™

AND THE KAIJU KERFUFFLE!

ONI
PRESS
PRESENTS

BROK
AND 1

EDITED BY
JAMES LUCAS JONES
& BESS PALLARES

BOTS™

KAIJU KERFUFFLE!

WRITTEN BY
J. TORRES

ART, LETTERING,
& DESIGN BY
SEAN DOVE

PUBLISHED BY ONI PRESS, INC.

JOE NOZEMACK, PUBLISHER

JAMES LUCAS JONES, EDITOR IN CHIEF

CHEYENNE ALLOTT, DIRECTOR OF SALES

AMBER O'NEILL, MARKETING COORDINATOR

RACHEL REED, PUBLICITY COORDINATOR

TROY LOOK, DIRECTOR OF DESIGN & PRODUCTION

HILARY THOMPSON, GRAPHIC DESIGNER

JARED JONES, DIGITAL ART TECHNICIAN

ARI YARWOOD, MANAGING EDITOR

CHARLIE CHU, SENIOR EDITOR

ROBIN HERRERA, EDITOR

BESS PALLARES, EDITORIAL ASSISTANT

BRAD ROOKS, DIRECTOR OF LOGISTICS

JUNG LEE, OFFICE ASSISTANT

ONIPRESS.COM

FACEBOOK.COM/ONIPRESS

TWITTER.COM/ONIPRESS

ONIPRESS.TUMBLR.COM

Find J. TORRES online at

FACEBOOK.COM/JTORRESCOMICS

@JTORRESCOMICS

Find SEAN DOVE online at

ANDTHANKYOUFORFLYING.COM

@ANDTHANKYOU

FIRST EDITION: MAY 2016

ISBN 978-1-62010-306-7
EISBN 978-1-62010-307-4

PRINTED IN CHINA

LIBRARY OF CONGRESS CONTROL NUMBER: 2015919324

1 2 3 4 5 6 7 8 9 10

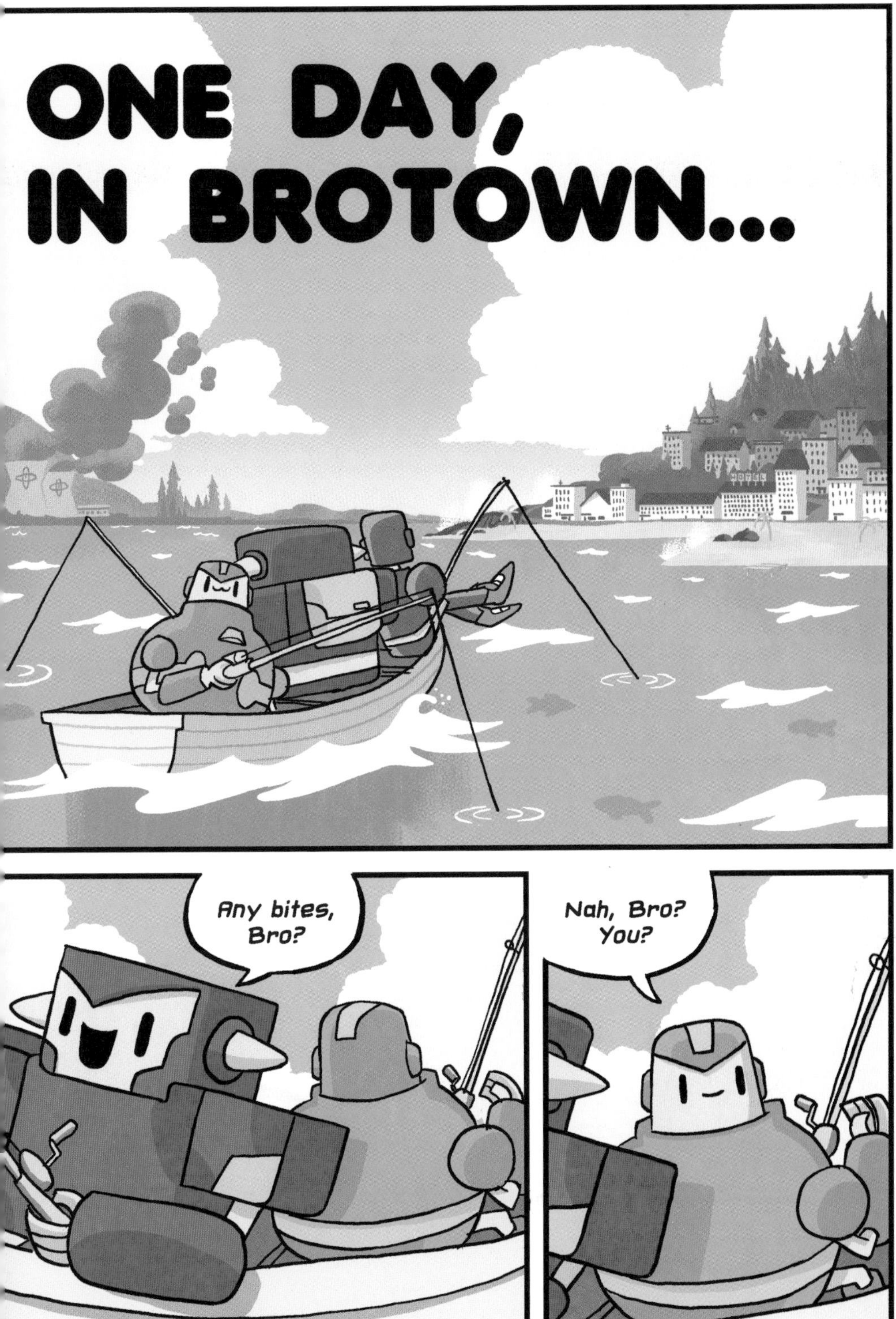
ONE DAY, IN BROTOWN...
HOTEL
Any bites, Bro?
Nah, Bro? You?

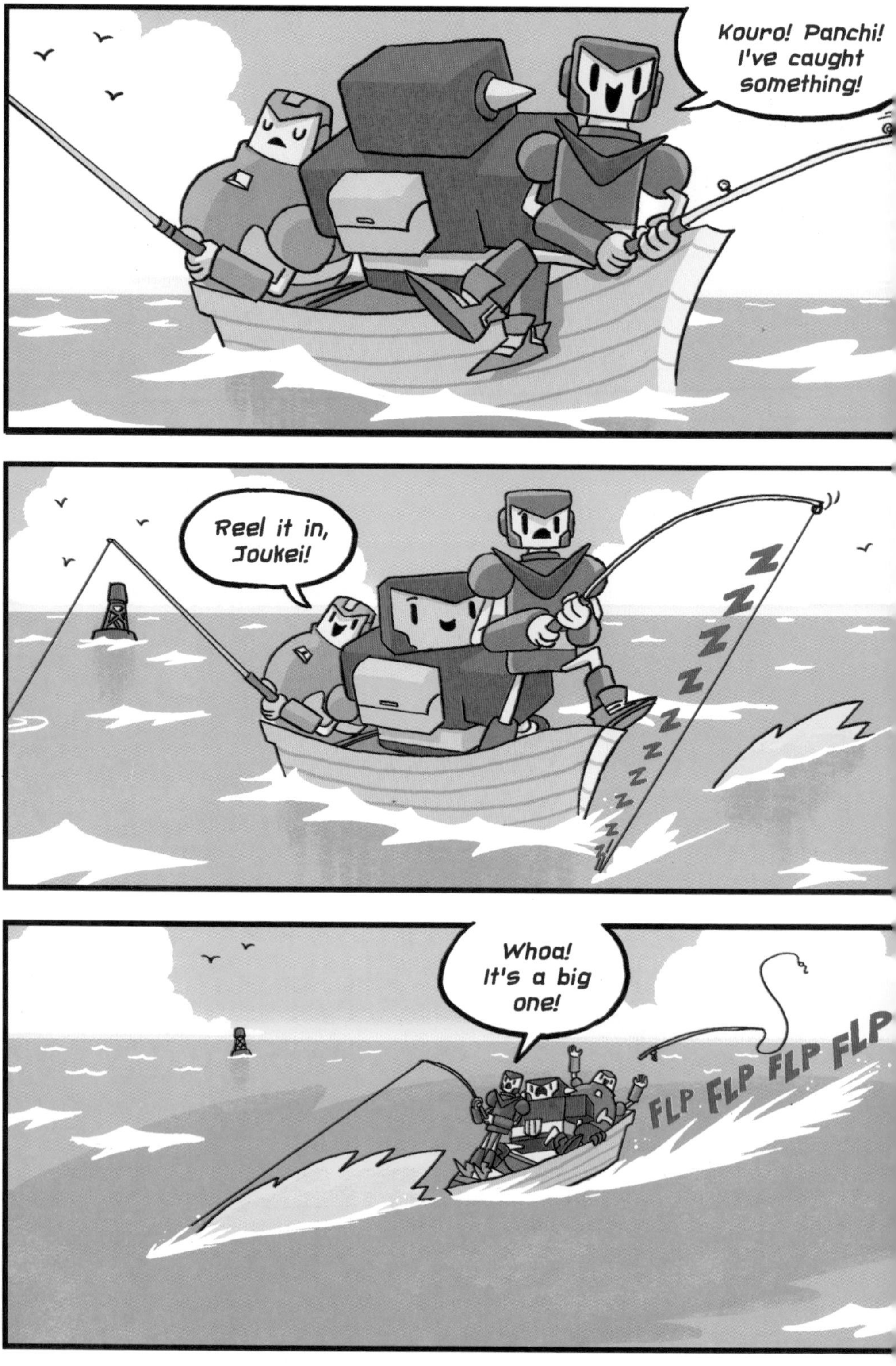
Kouro! Panchi! I've caught something!
Reel it in, Joukei!
Whoa! It's a big one!
FLP FLP FLP FLP

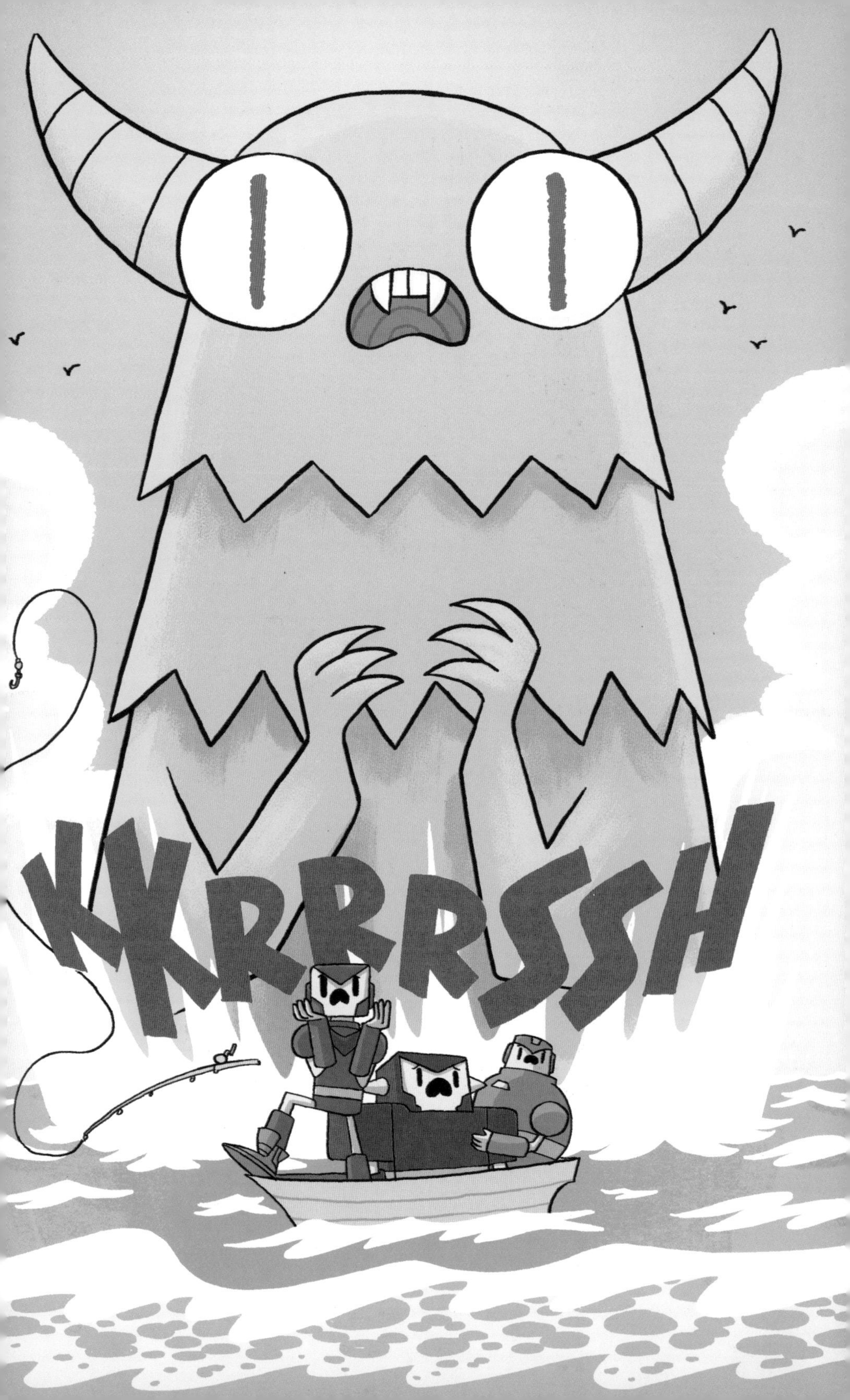
KRRRSSH

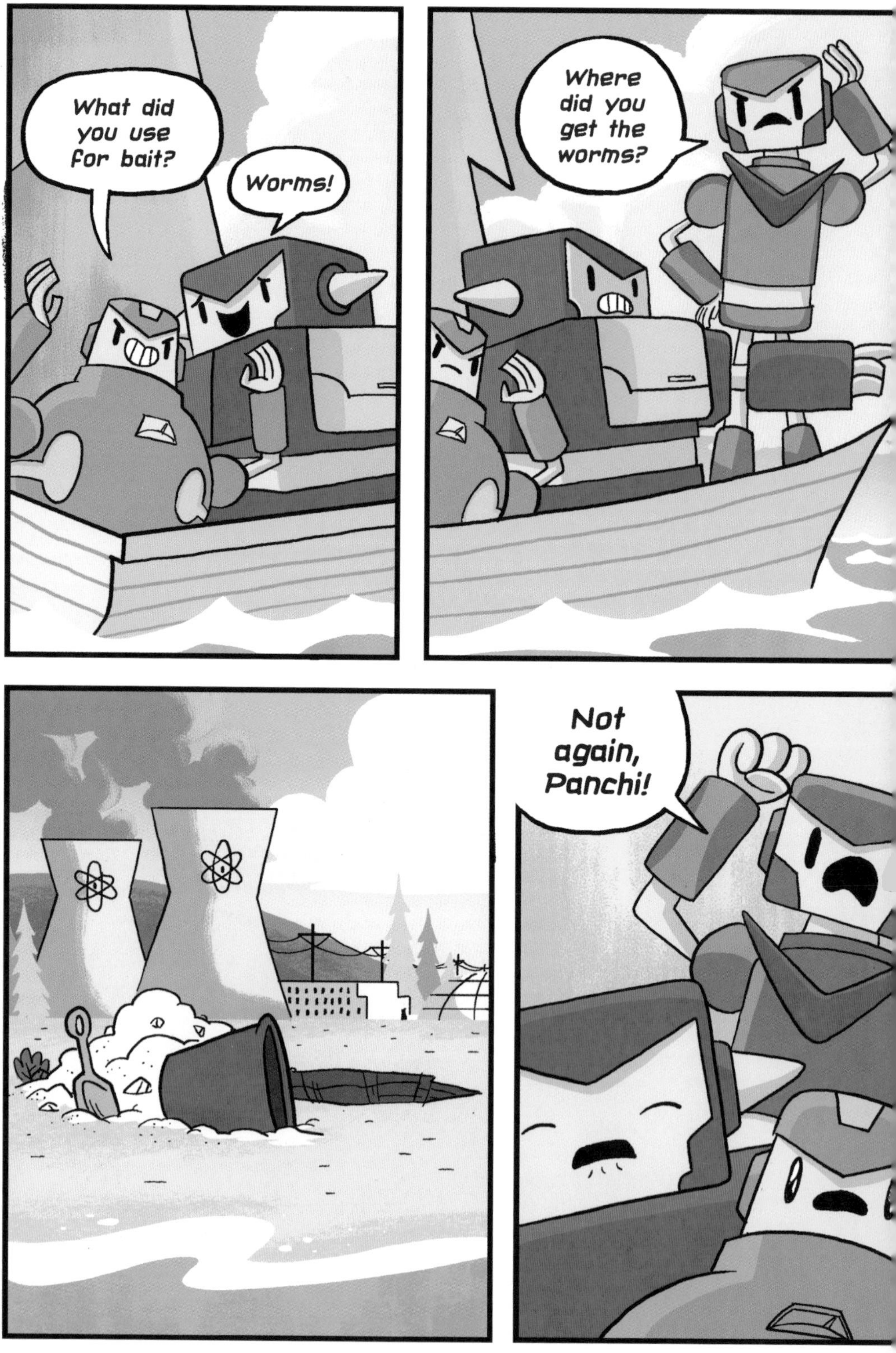
What did you use for bait?
Worms!
Where did you get the worms?
Not again, Panchi!

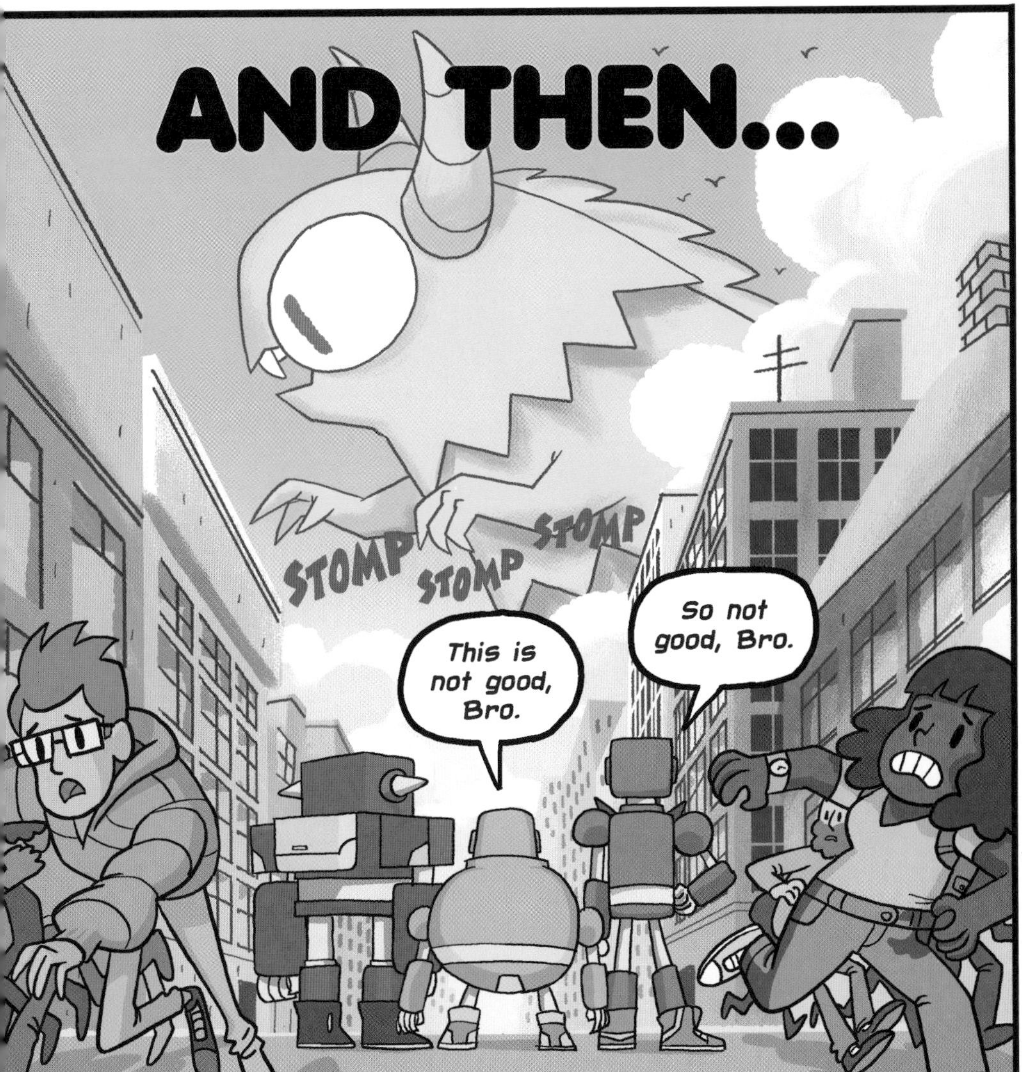
AND THEN...
STOMP
STOMP
STOMP
This is not good, Bro.
So not good, Bro.

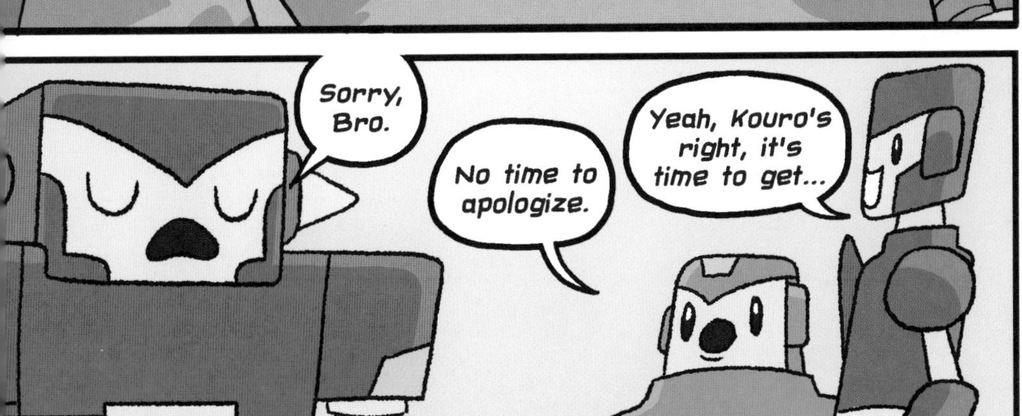
Sorry, Bro.
No time to apologize.
Yeah, Kouro's right, it's time to get...

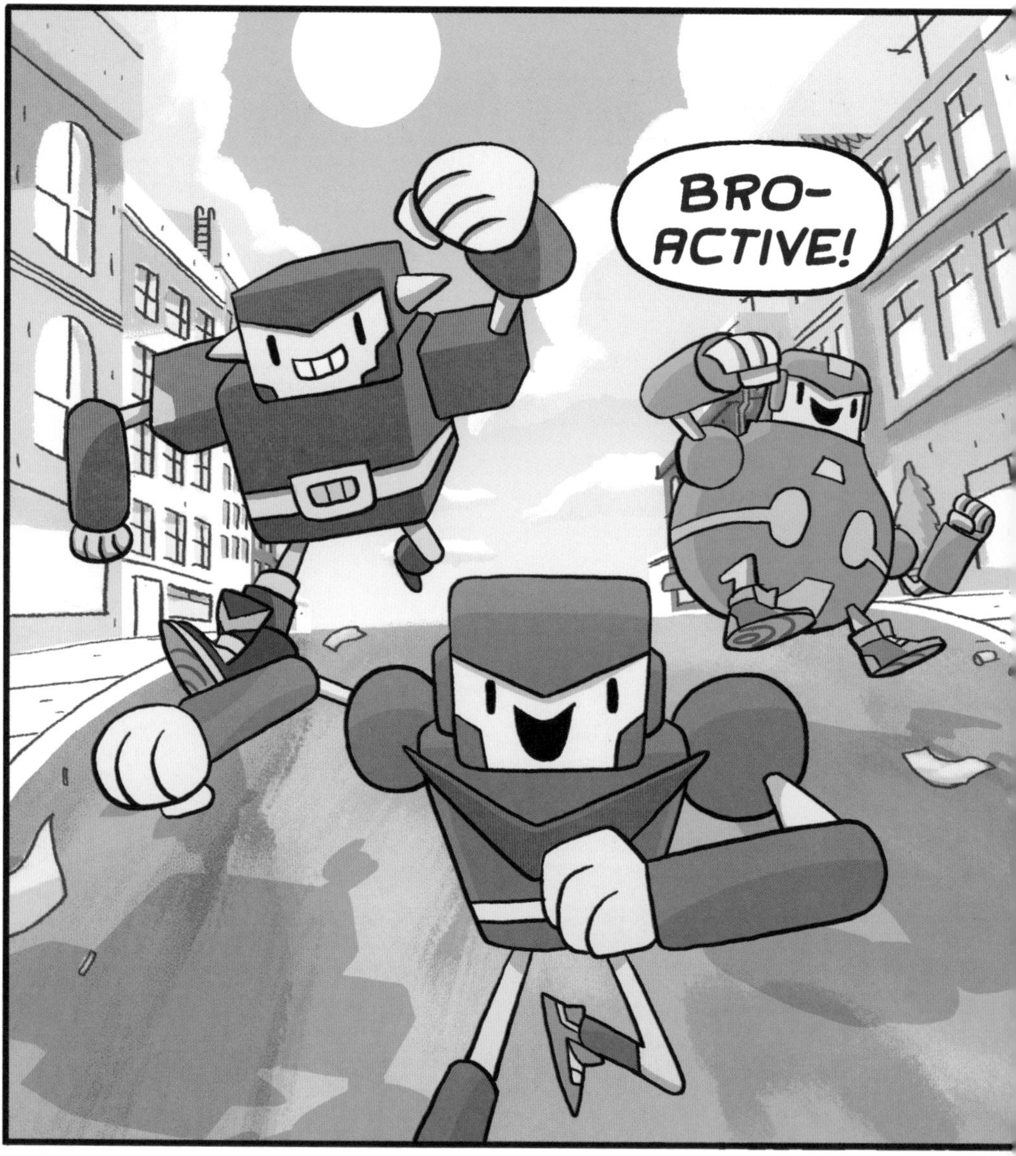
BRO-
ACTIVE!

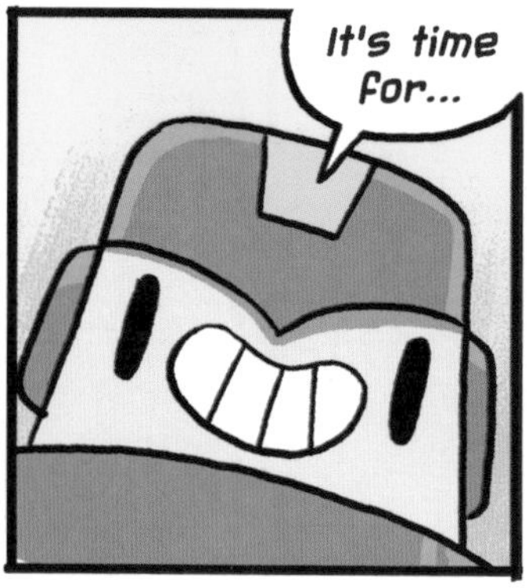
It's time for...

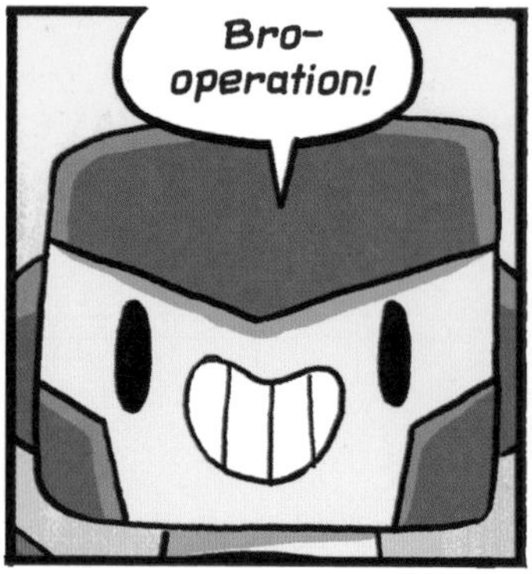
Bro-operation!

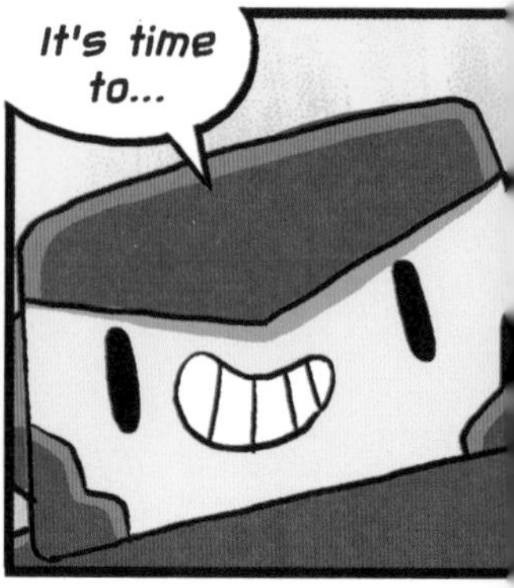
It's time to...

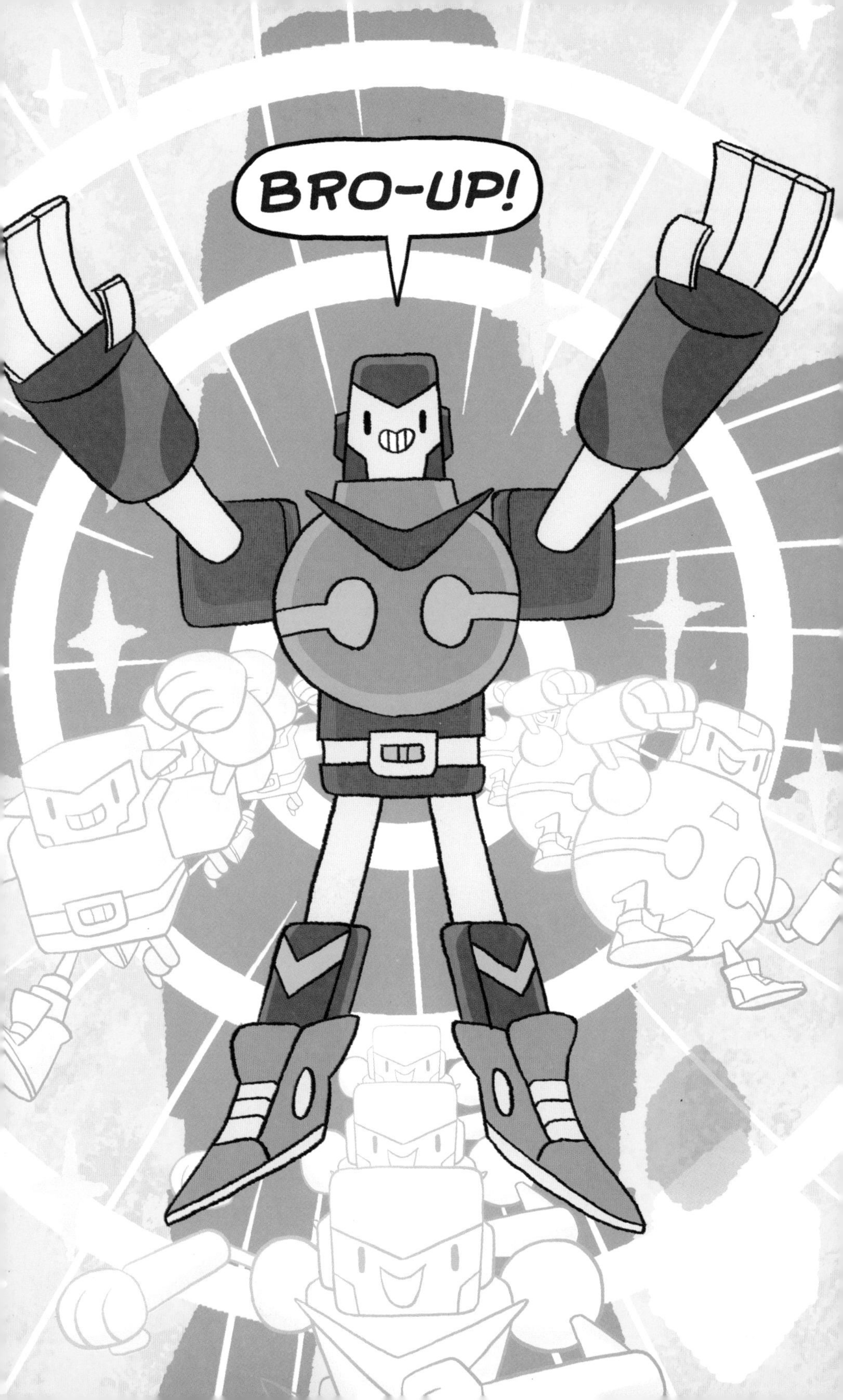
BRO-UP!

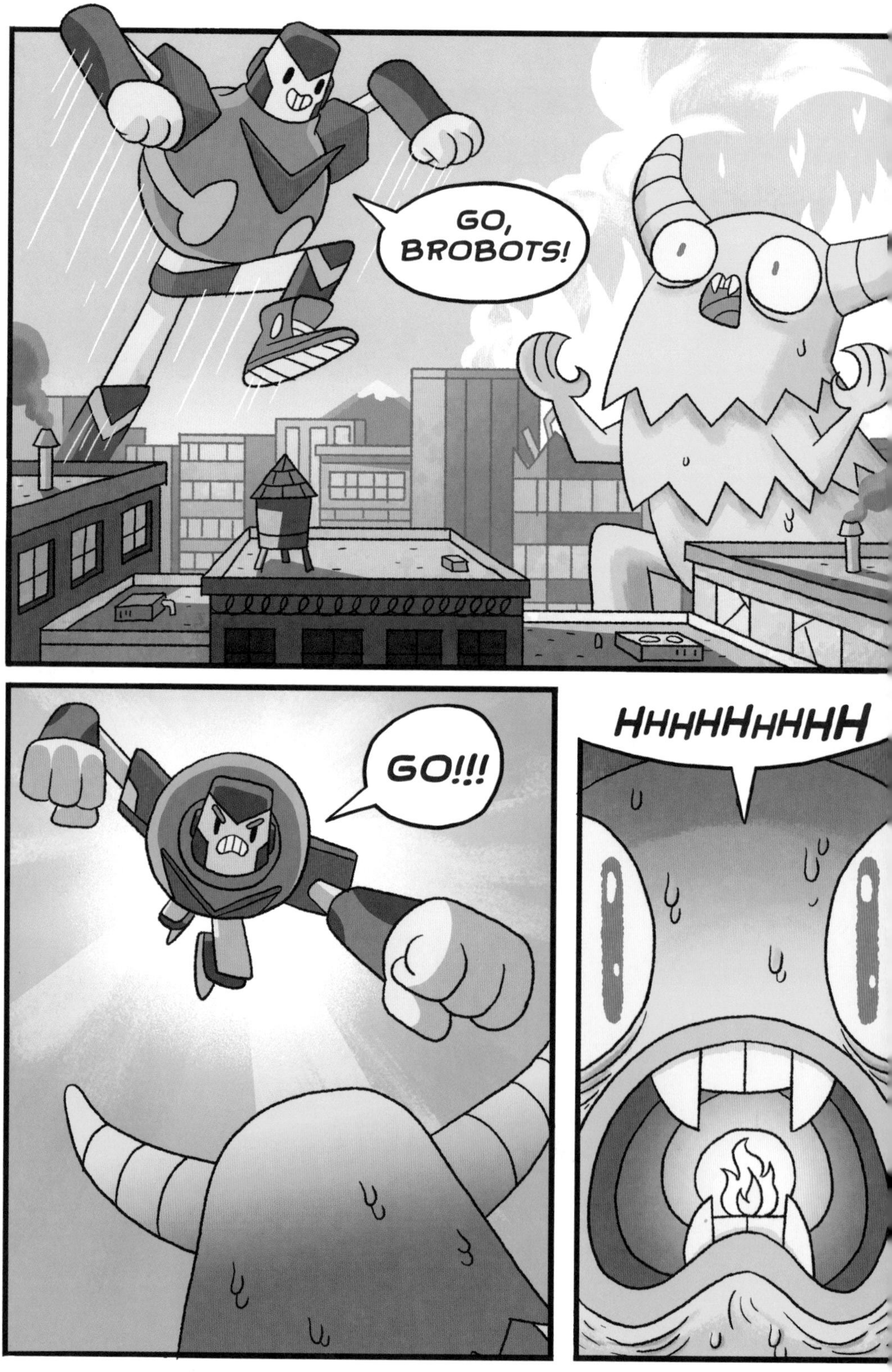
GO, BROBOTS!
GO!!!
HHHHHHHHH

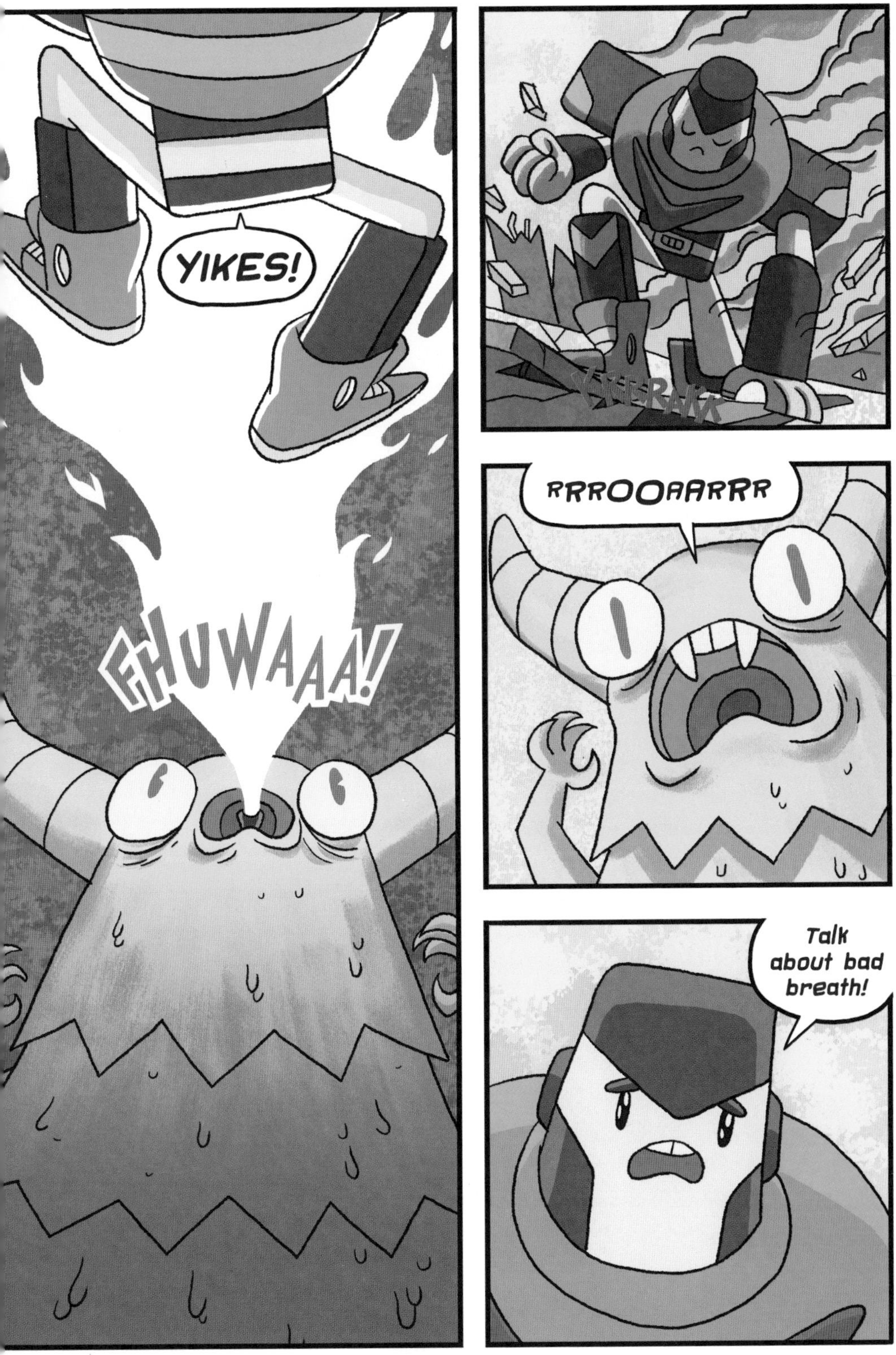
YIKES!
FHUWAAA!
RRROOAARRR
Talk about bad breath!

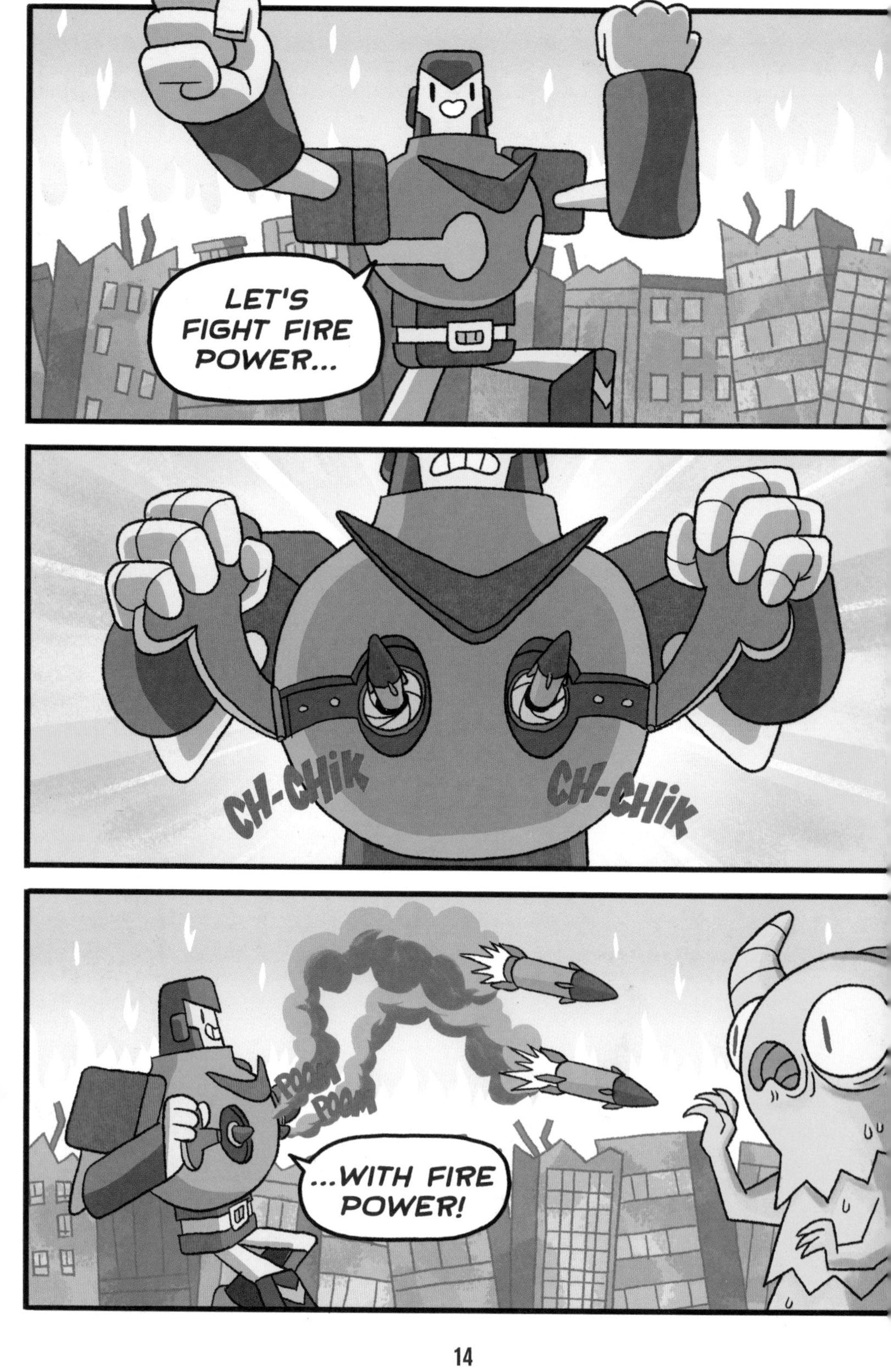
LET'S FIGHT FIRE POWER...
CH-CHIK
CH-CHIK
POOM
POOM
...WITH FIRE POWER!

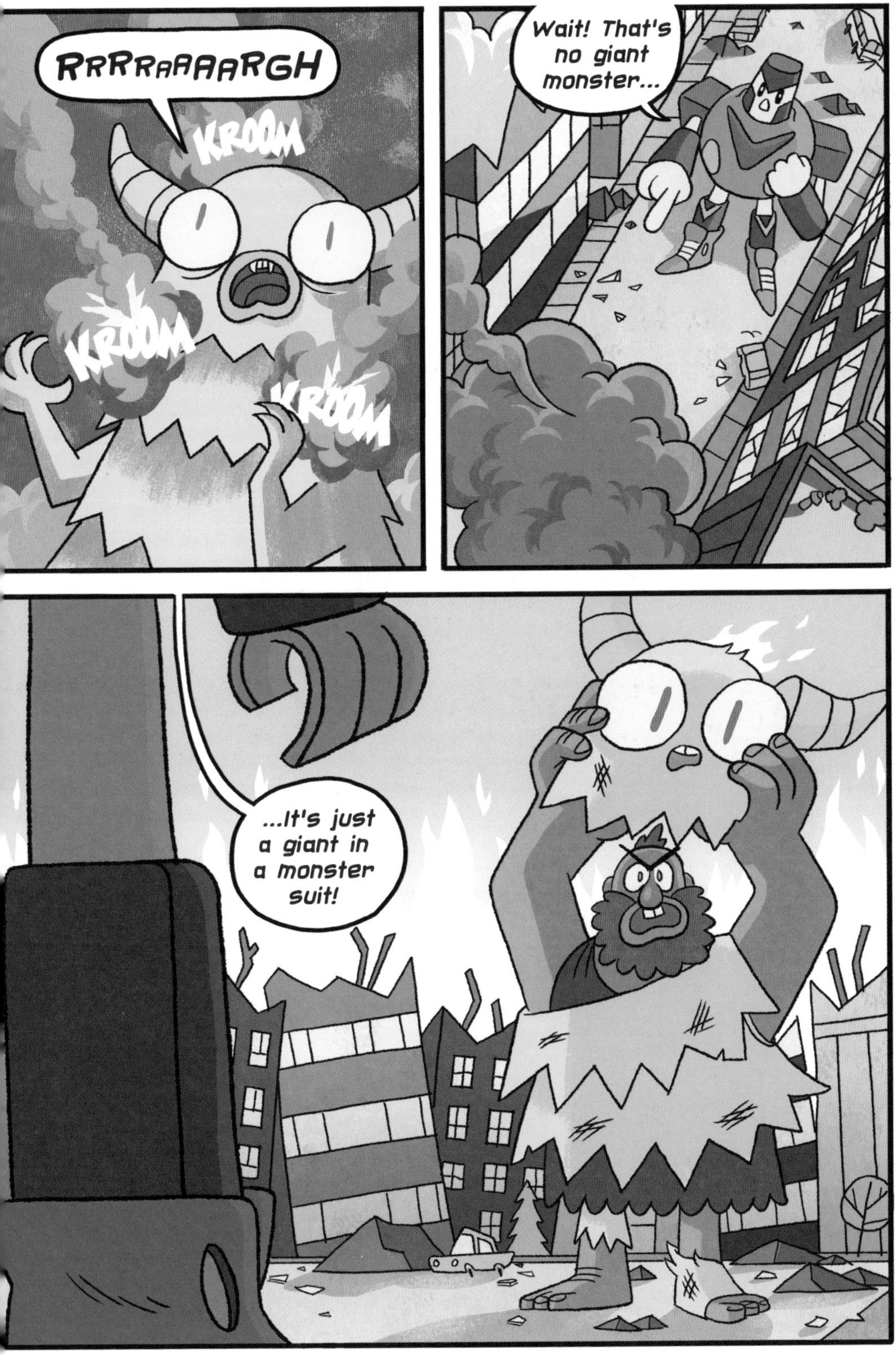
RRRRAAAARGH
KROOM
KROOM
KROOM
Wait! That's no giant monster...
...It's just a giant in a monster suit!

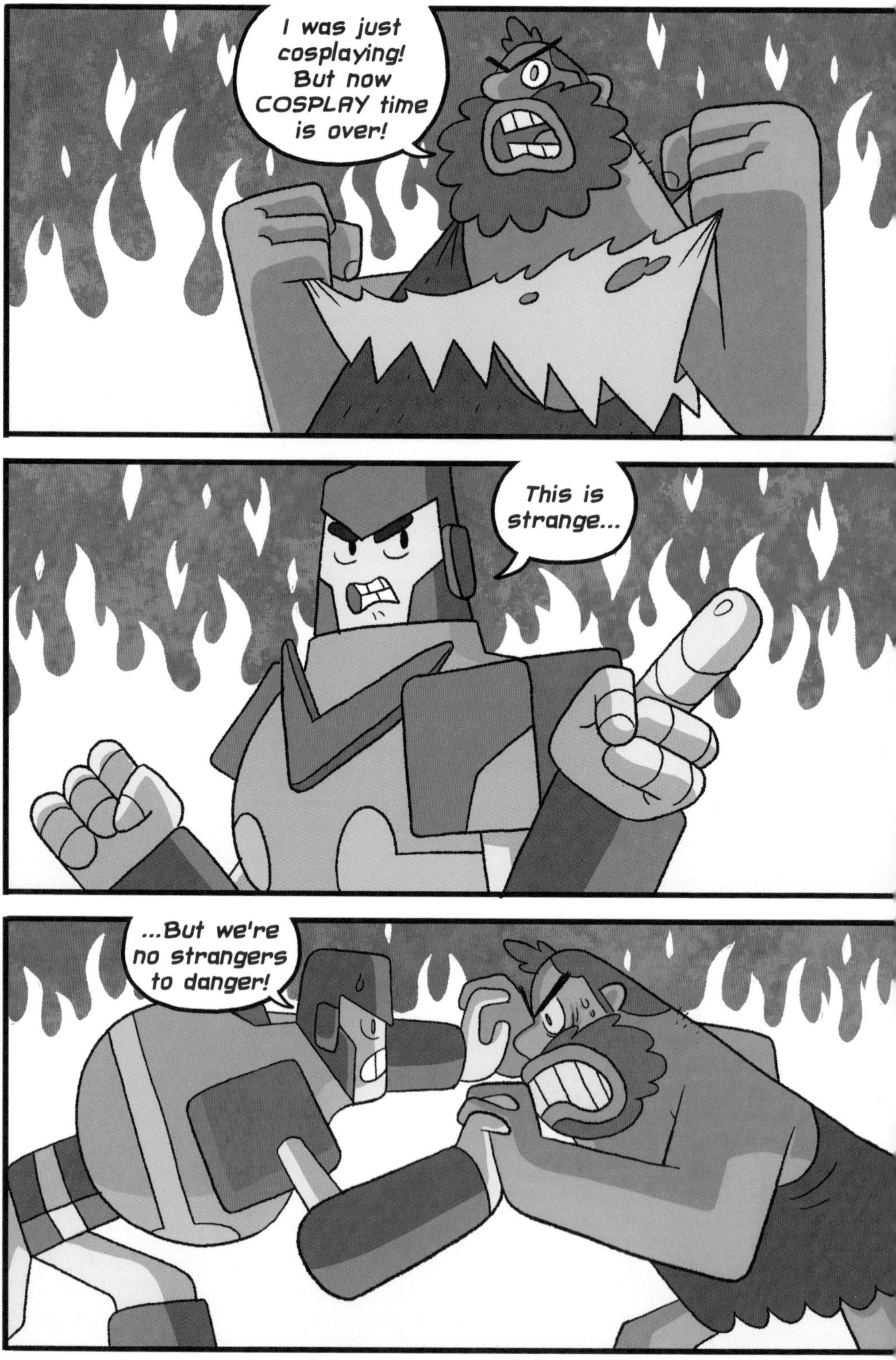
I was just cosplaying! But now COSPLAY time is over!
This is strange...
...But we're no strangers to danger!

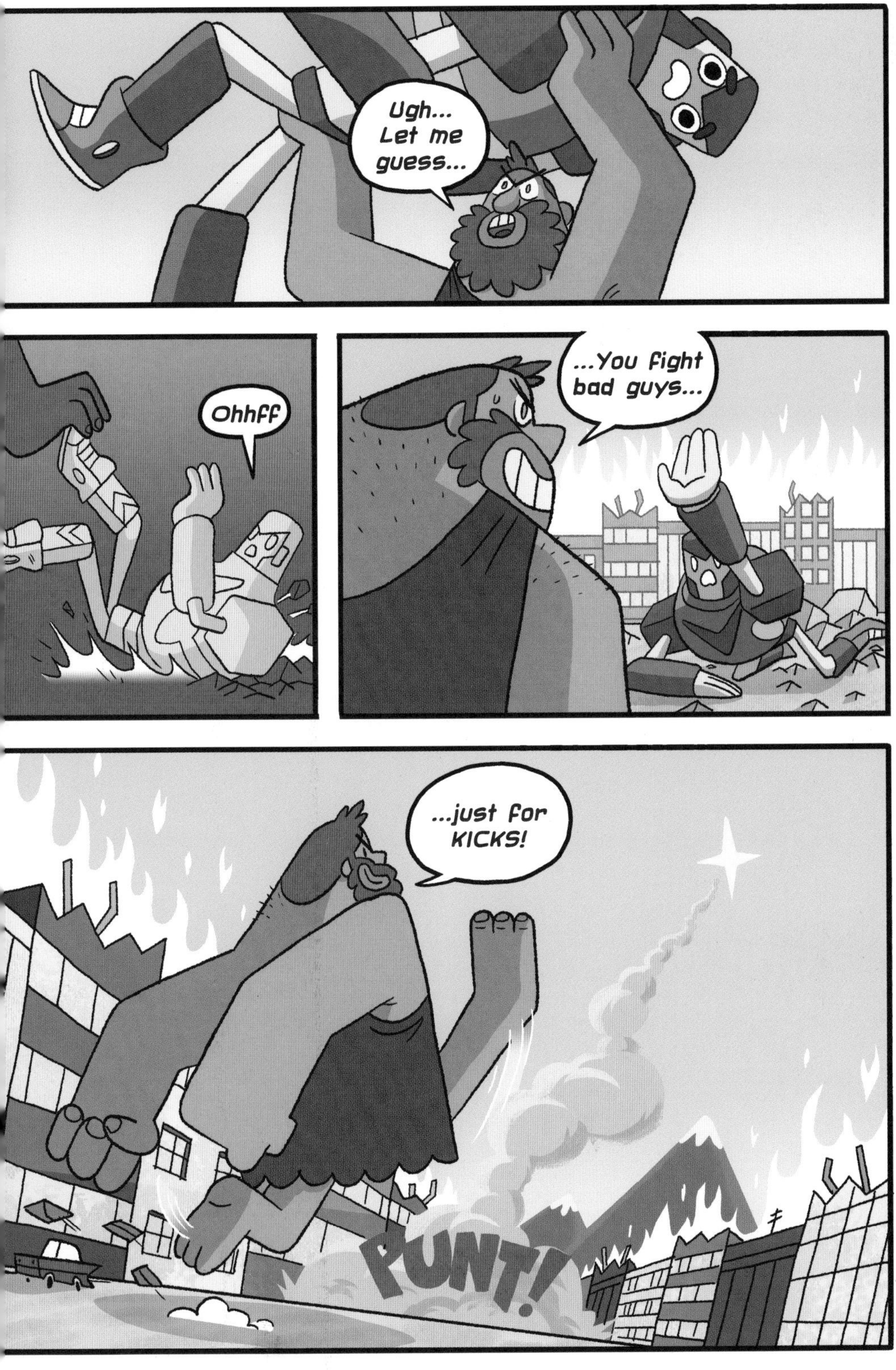
Ugh... Let me guess...
Ohhff
...You fight bad guys...
...just for KICKS!
PUNT!

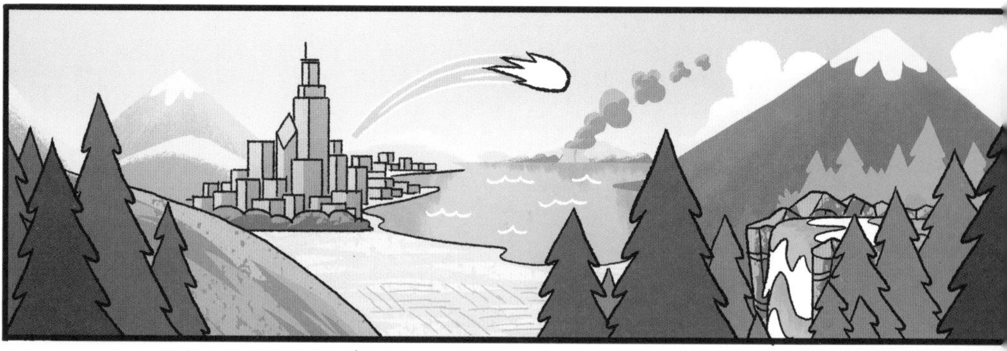

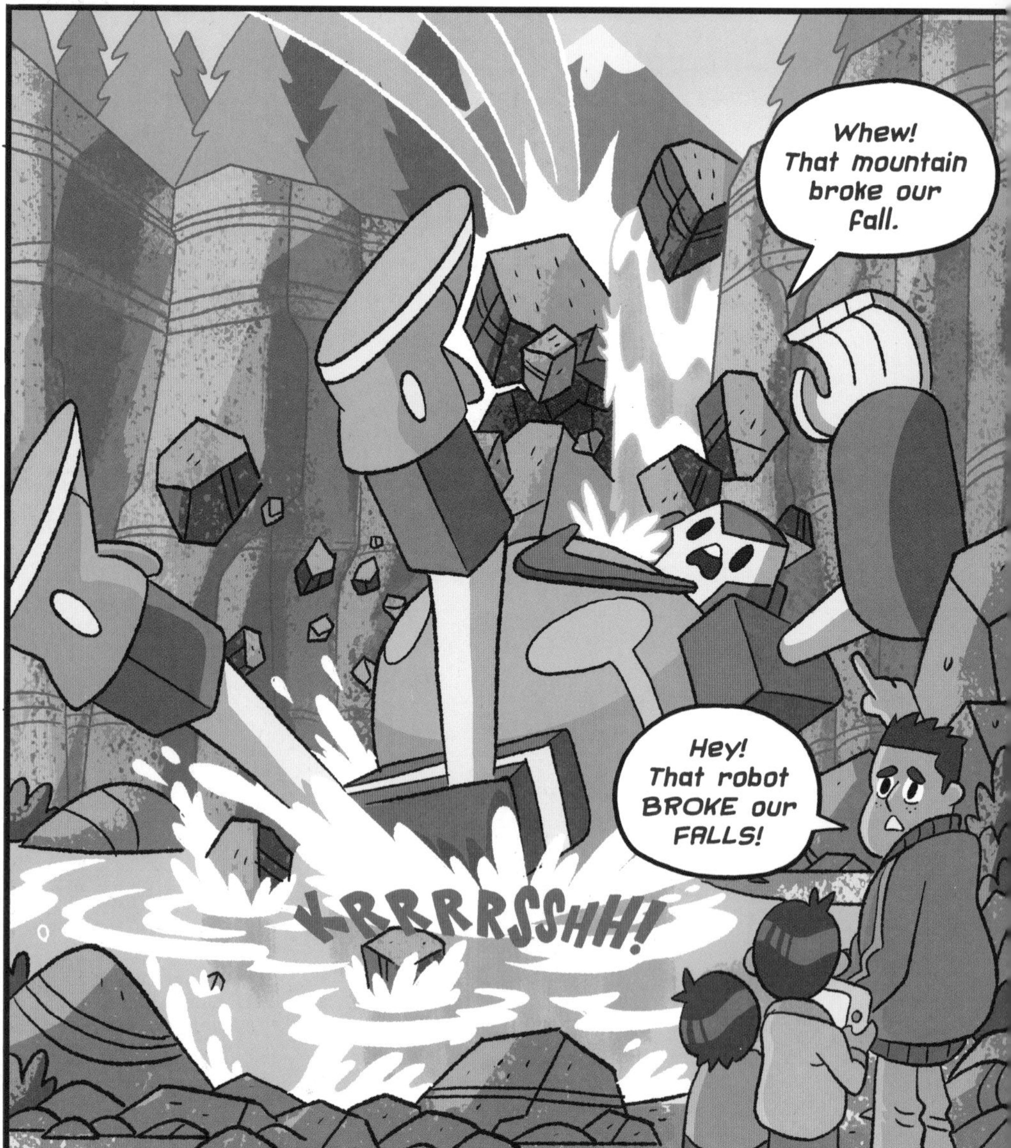
Whew! That mountain broke our fall.
Hey! That robot BROKE our FALLS!
KRRRRRSSHH!

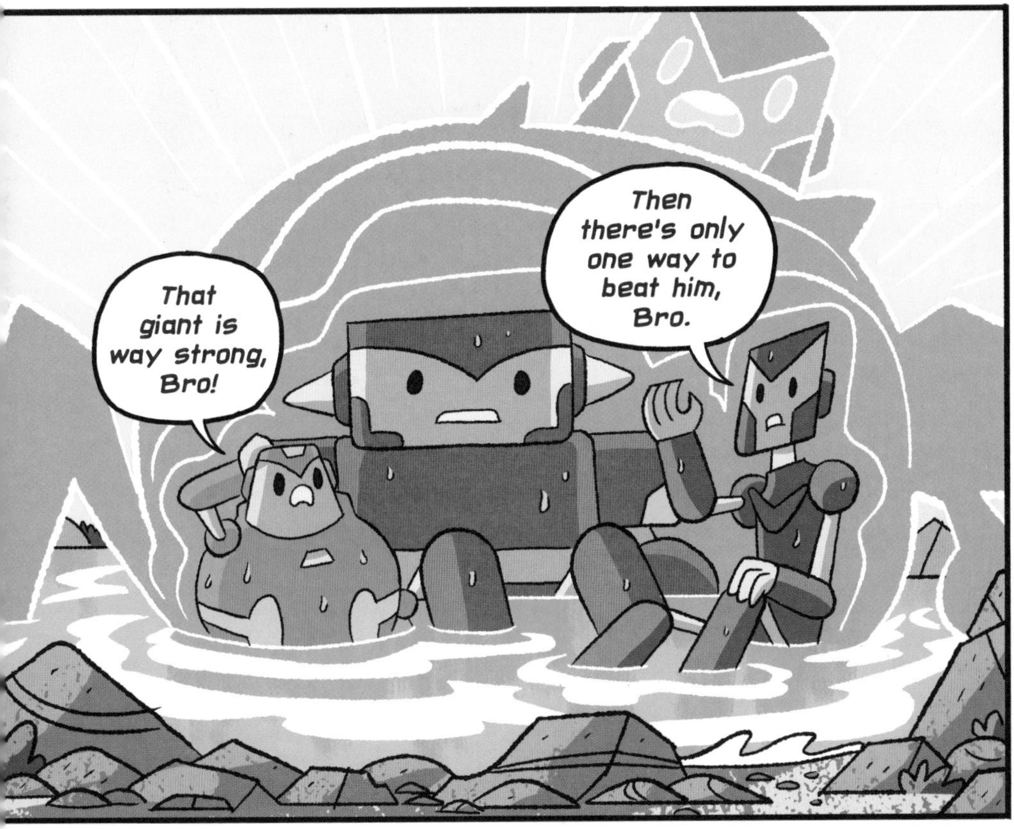
That giant is way strong, Bro!
Then there's only one way to beat him, Bro.

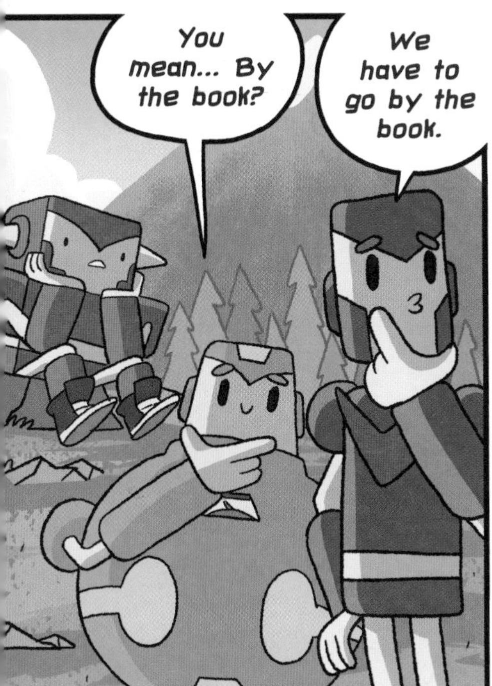
You mean... By the book?
We have to go by the book.

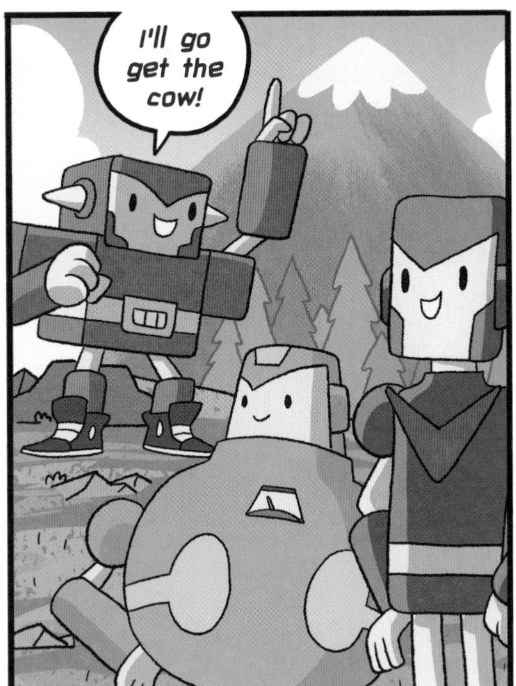
I'll go get the cow!

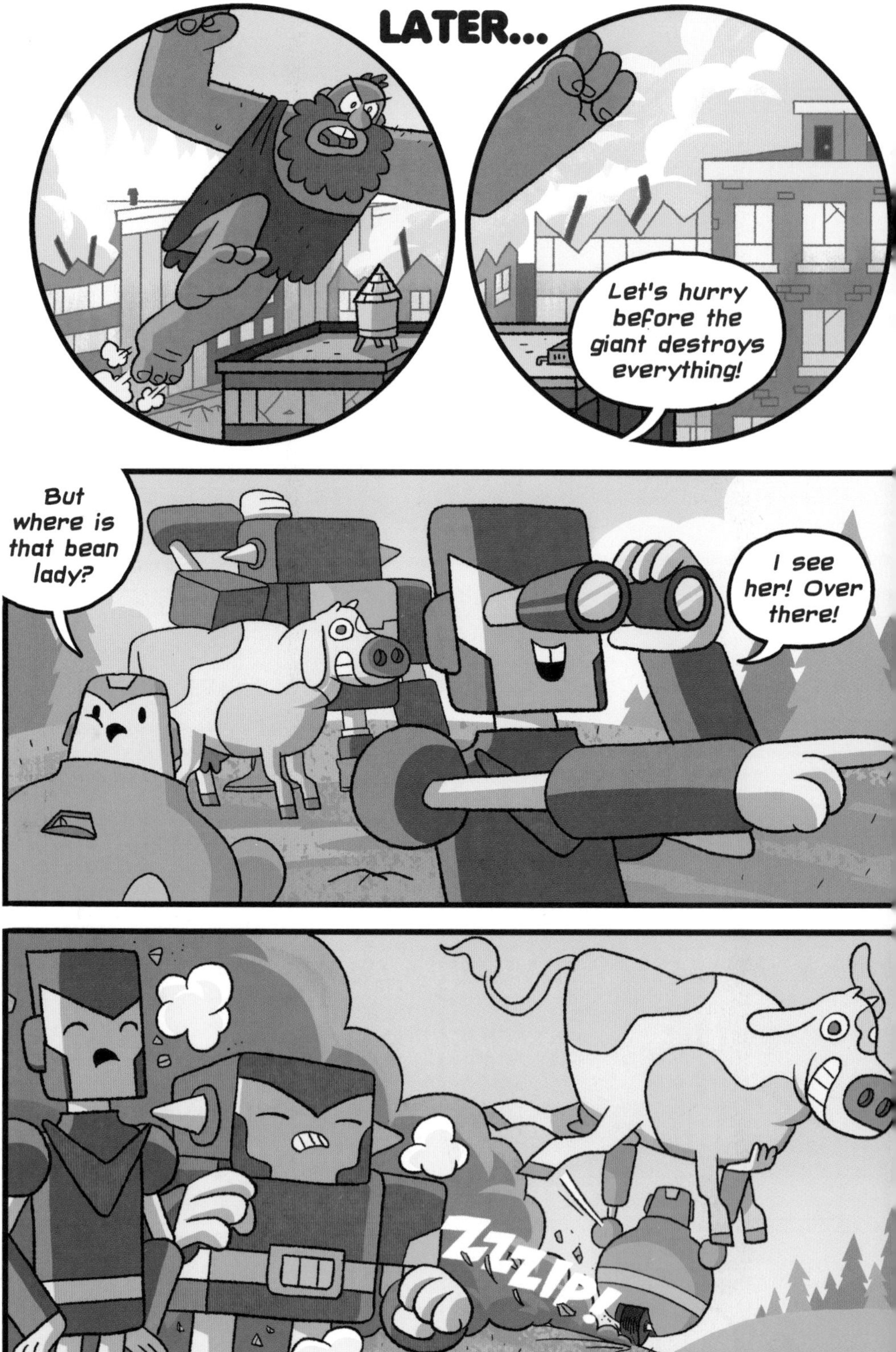
LATER...
Let's hurry before the giant destroys everything!
But where is that bean lady?
I see her! Over there!
ZZZIP!

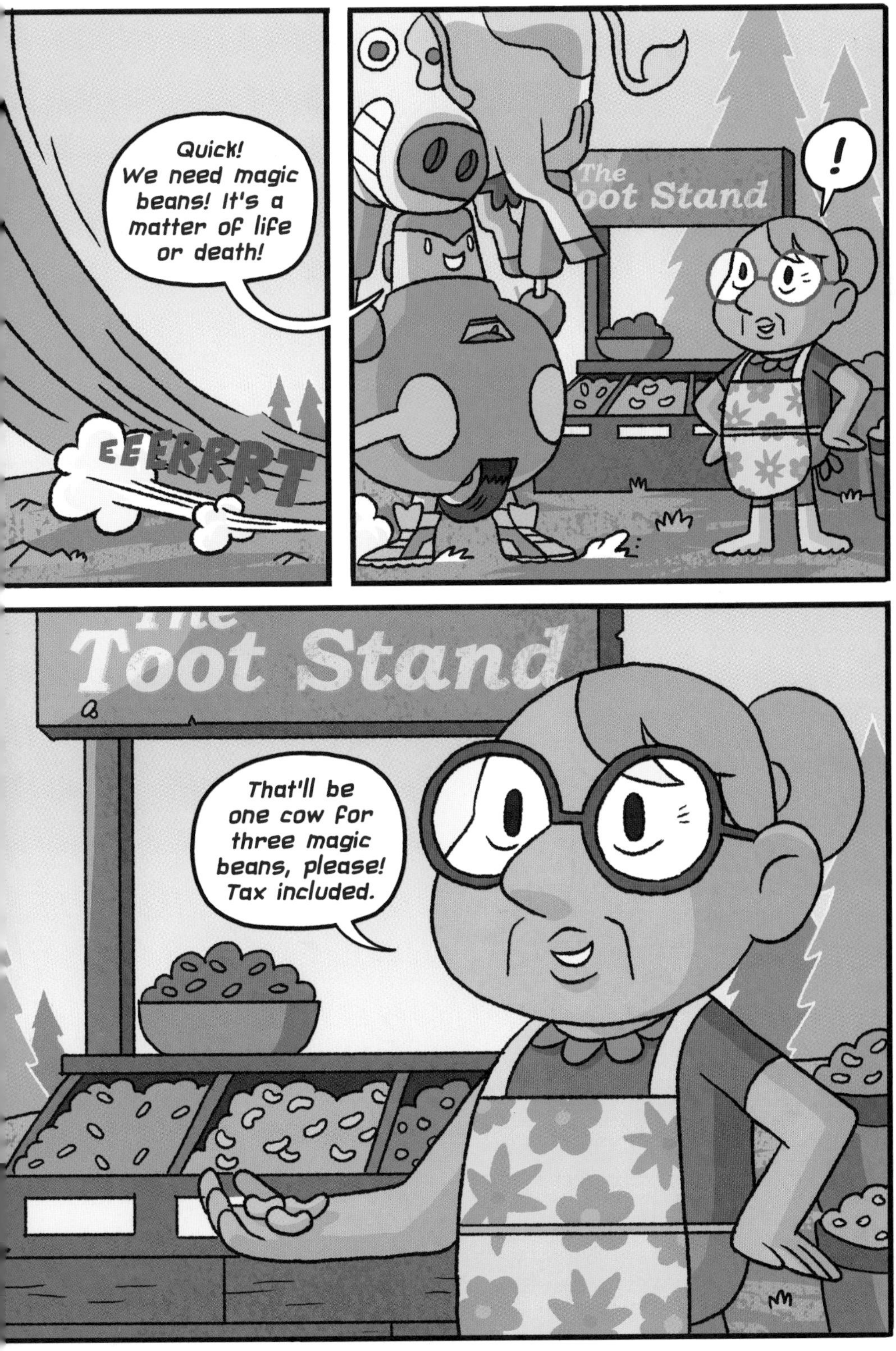
Quick! We need magic beans! It's a matter of life or death!
EEERRRRT
The Toot Stand
!
Toot Stand
That'll be one cow for three magic beans, please! Tax included.

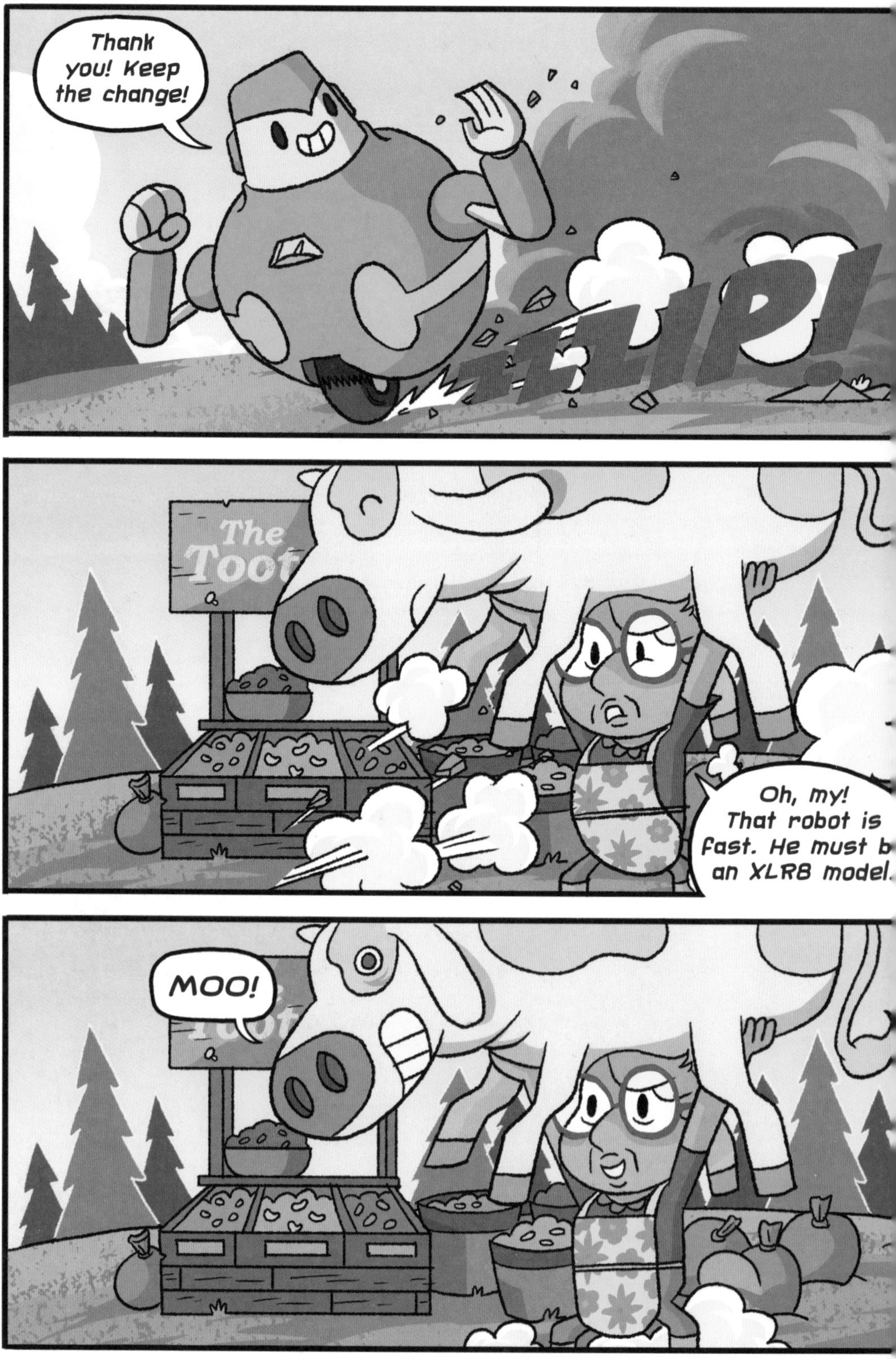
Thank you! Keep the change!
ZZIP!
The Toot
Oh, my! That robot is fast. He must b an XLR8 model.
MOO!

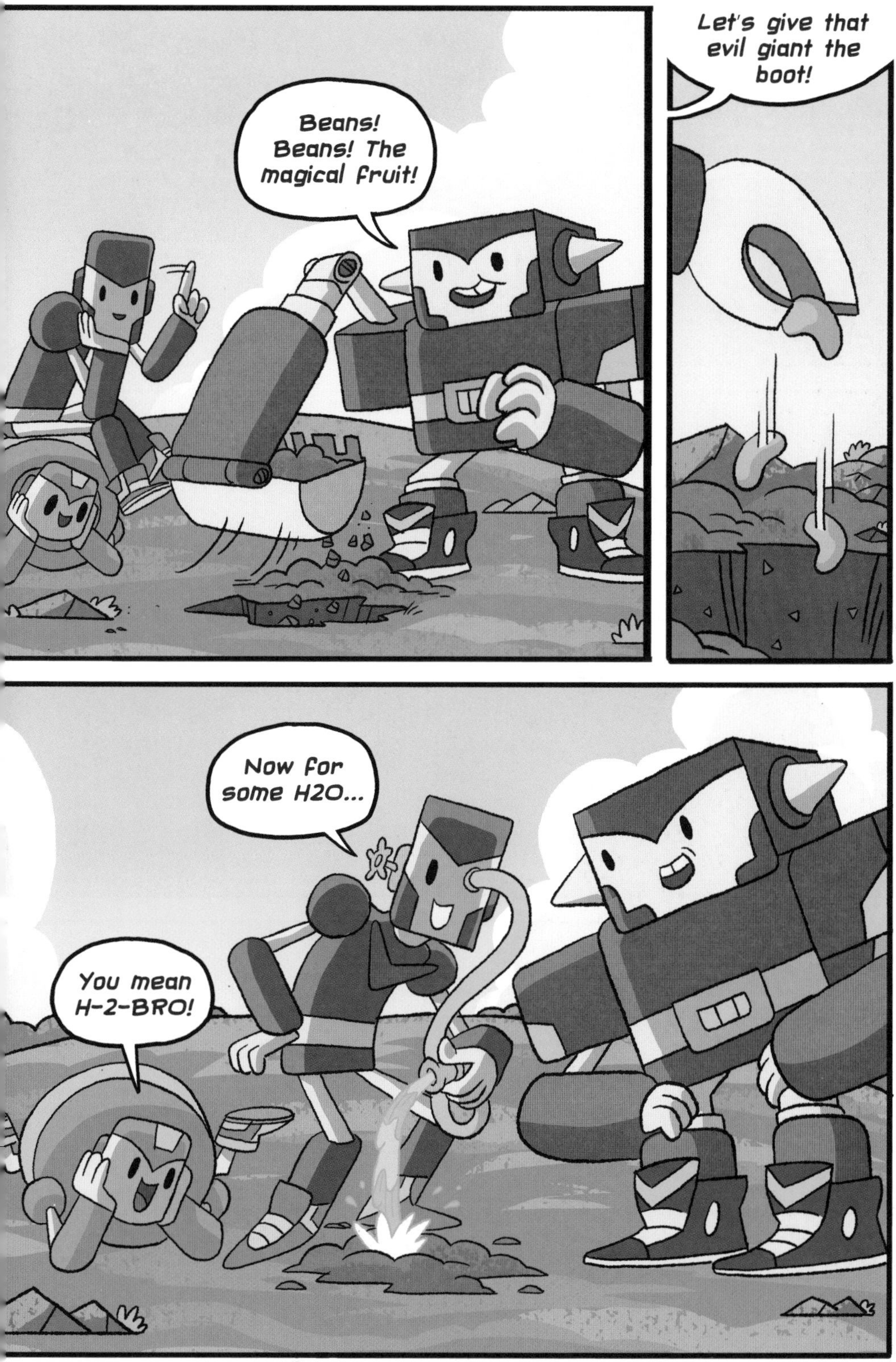
Beans! Beans! The magical fruit!
Let's give that evil giant the boot!
Now for some H2O...
You mean H-2-BRO!

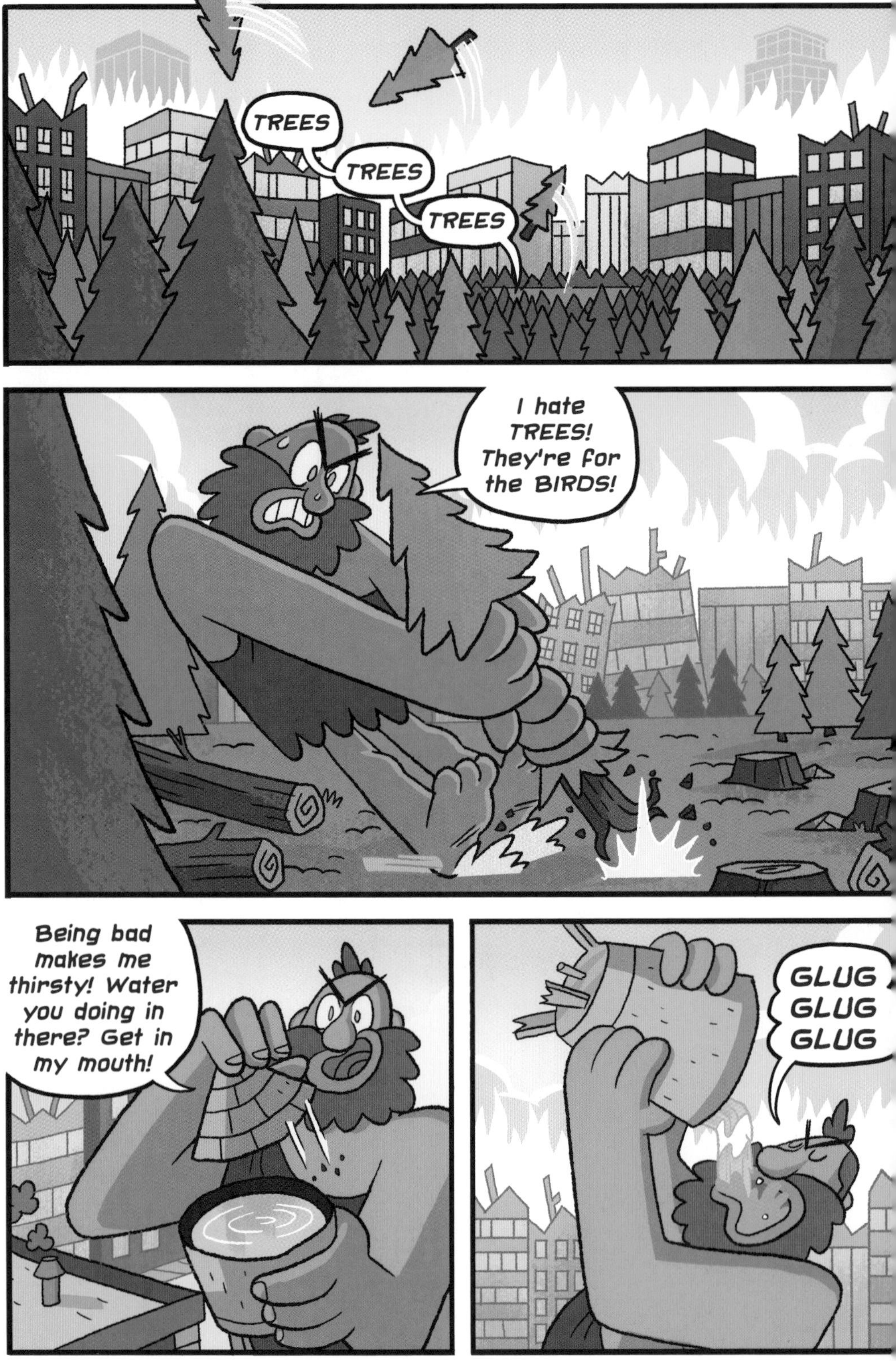
TREES
TREES
TREES
I hate TREES! They're for the BIRDS!
Being bad makes me thirsty! Water you doing in there? Get in my mouth!
GLUG GLUG GLUG

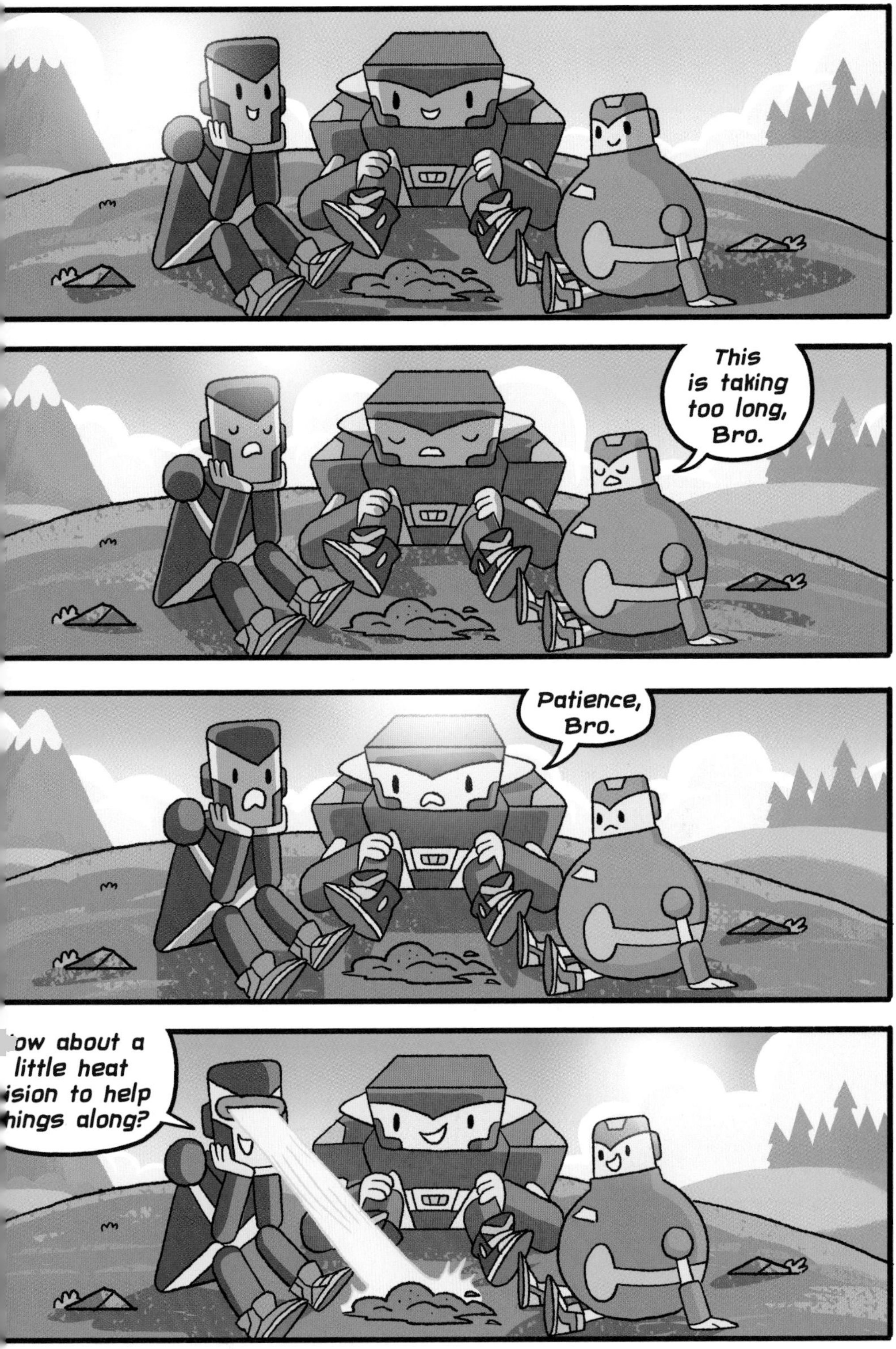
This is taking too long, Bro.
Patience, Bro.
ow about a little heat ision to help hings along?

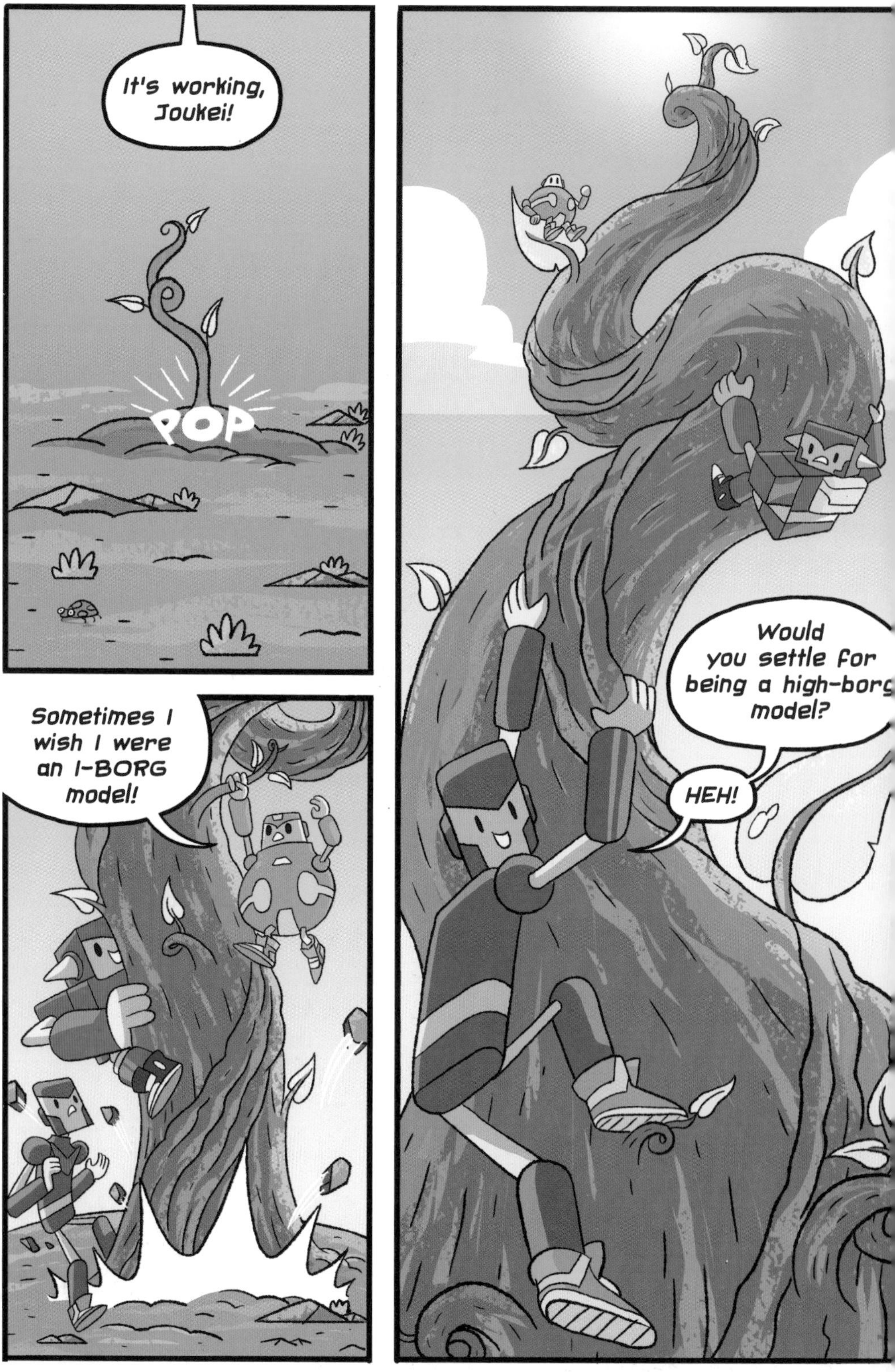
It's working, Joukei!
POP
Sometimes I wish I were an I-BORG model!
Would you settle for being a high-borg model?
HEH!

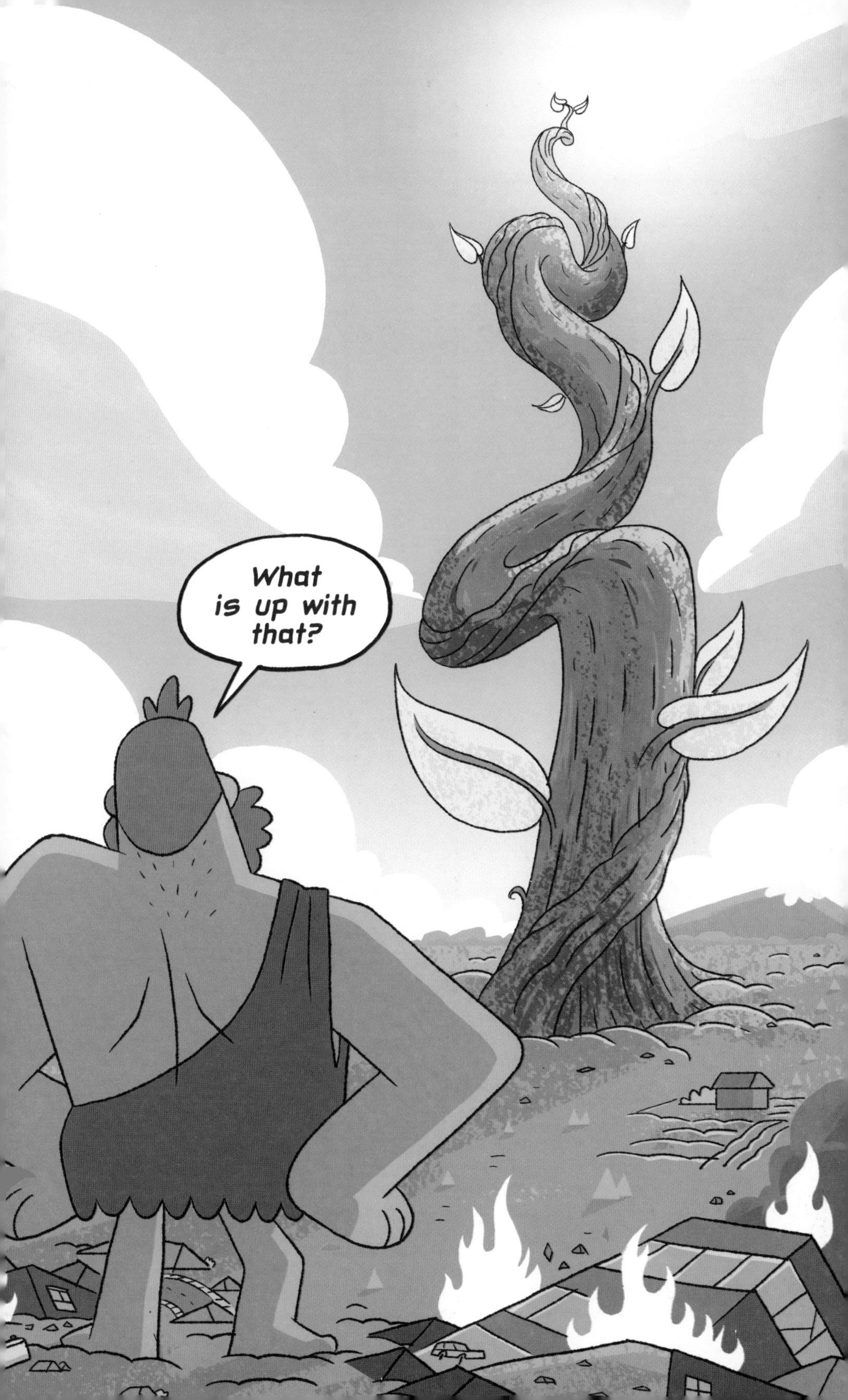
What is up with that?

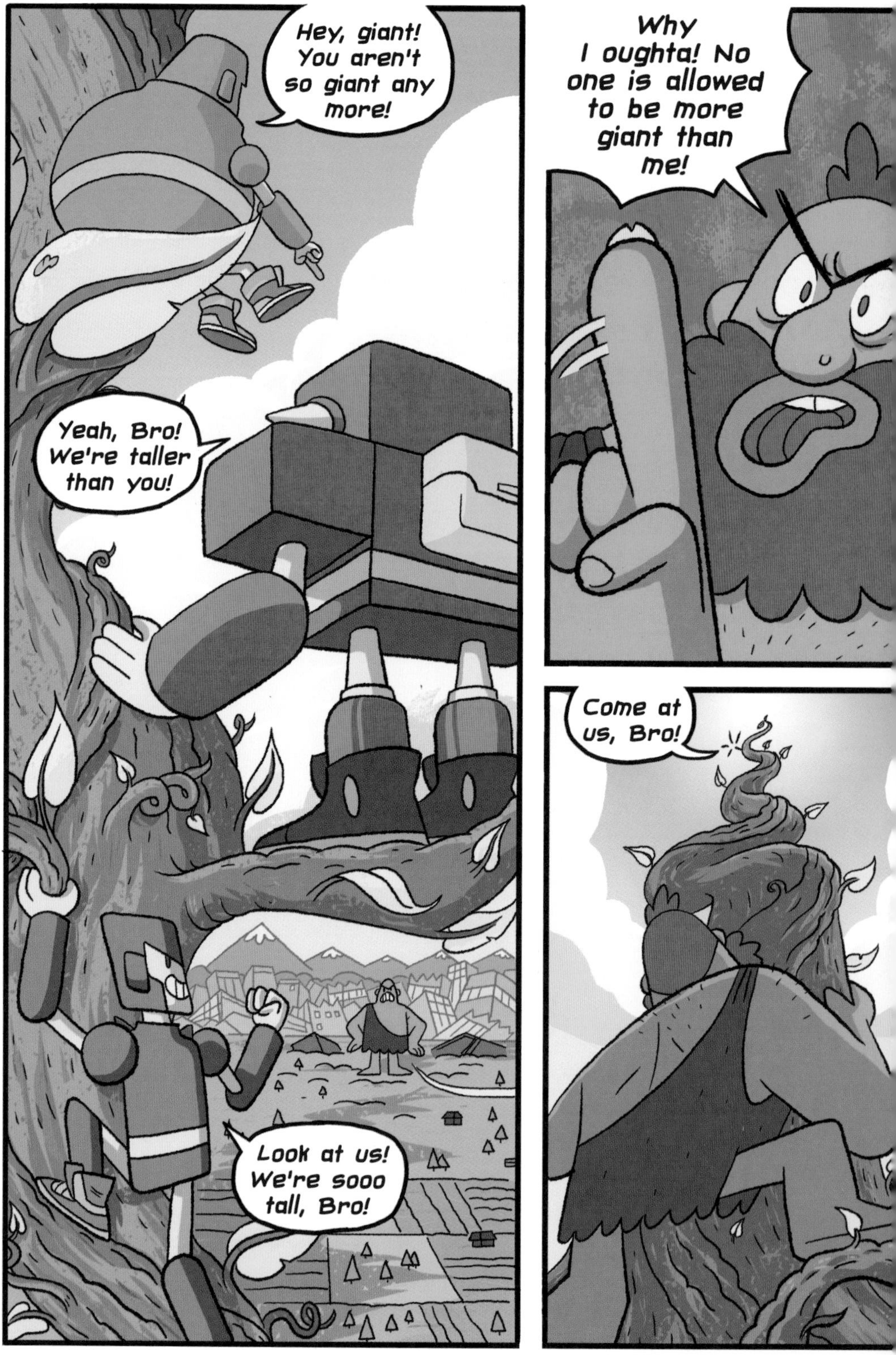
Hey, giant! You aren't so giant any more!
Yeah, Bro! We're taller than you!
Look at us! We're sooo tall, Bro!
Why I oughta! No one is allowed to be more giant than me!
Come at us, Bro!

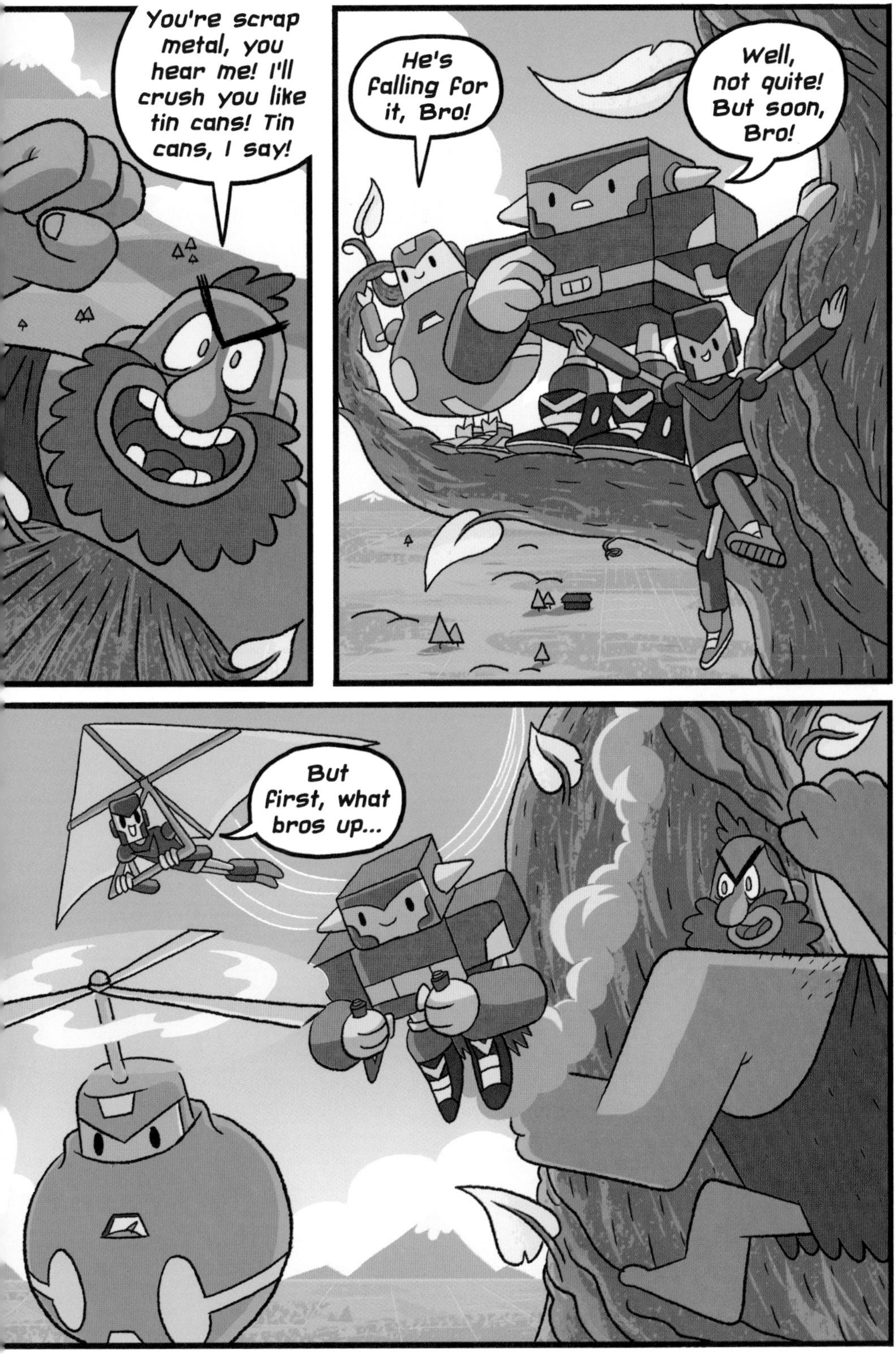
You're scrap metal, you hear me! I'll crush you like tin cans! Tin cans, I say!
He's falling for it, Bro!
Well, not quite! But soon, Bro!
But first, what bros up...

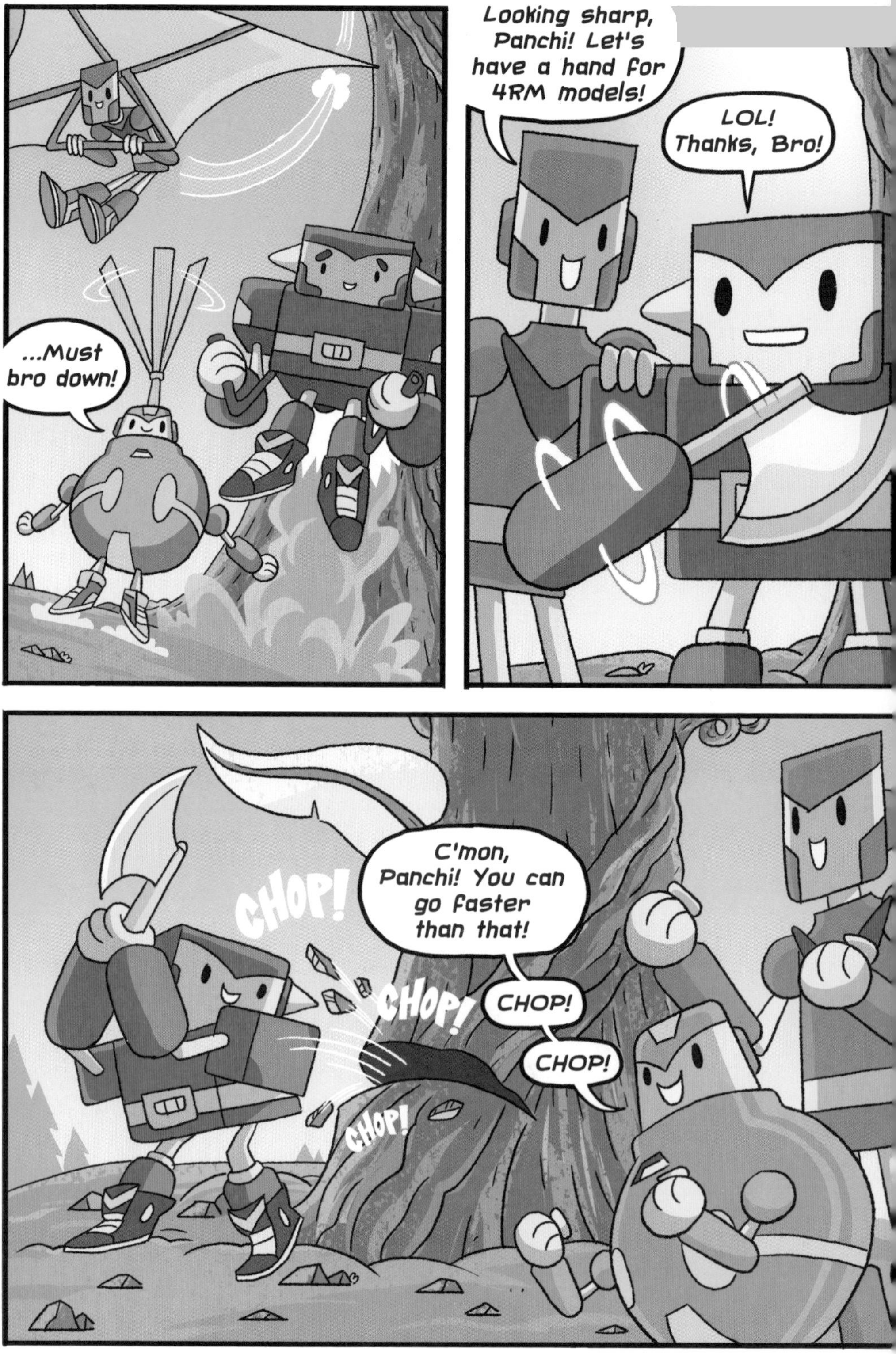
...Must bro down!
Looking sharp, Panchi! Let's have a hand for 4RM models!
LOL! Thanks, Bro!
CHOP!
C'mon, Panchi! You can go faster than that!
CHOP!
CHOP!
CHOP!
CHOP!

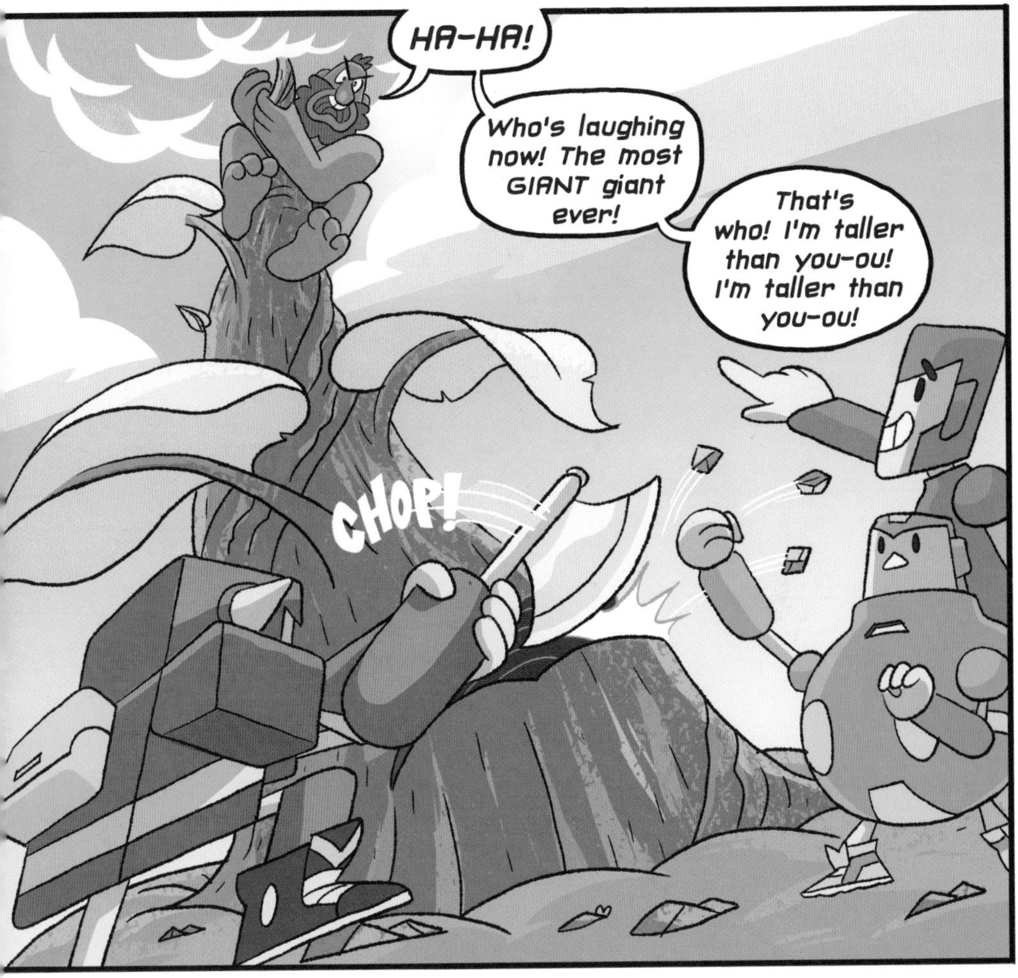
HA-HA!
Who's laughing now! The most GIANT giant ever!
That's who! I'm taller than you-ou! I'm taller than you-ou!
CHOP!

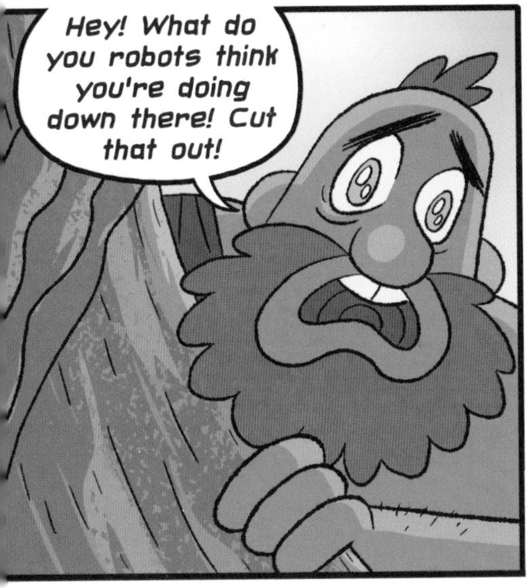
Hey! What do you robots think you're doing down there! Cut that out!

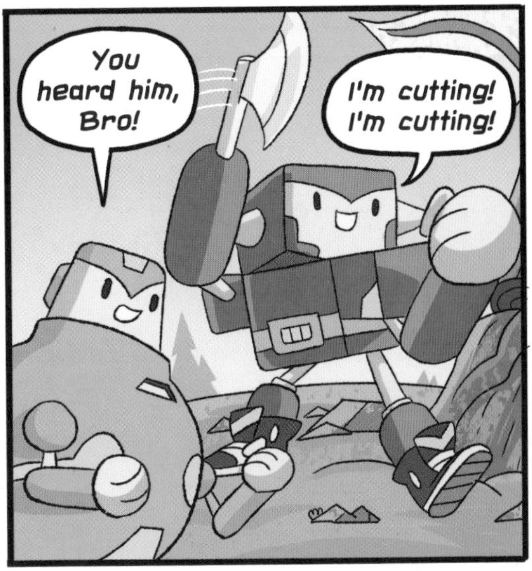
You heard him, Bro!
I'm cutting! I'm cutting!

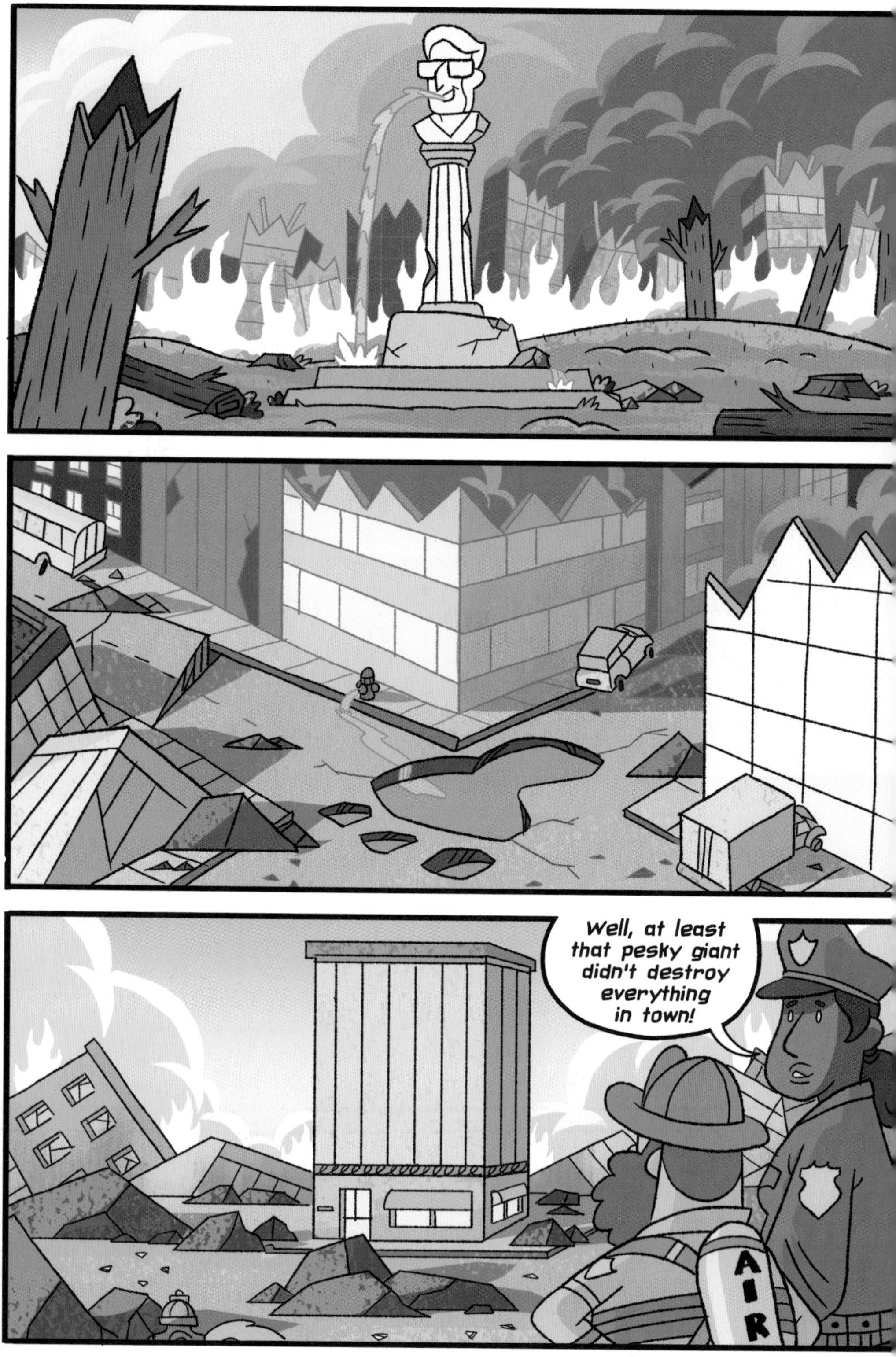
Well, at least that pesky giant didn't destroy everything in town!
AIR

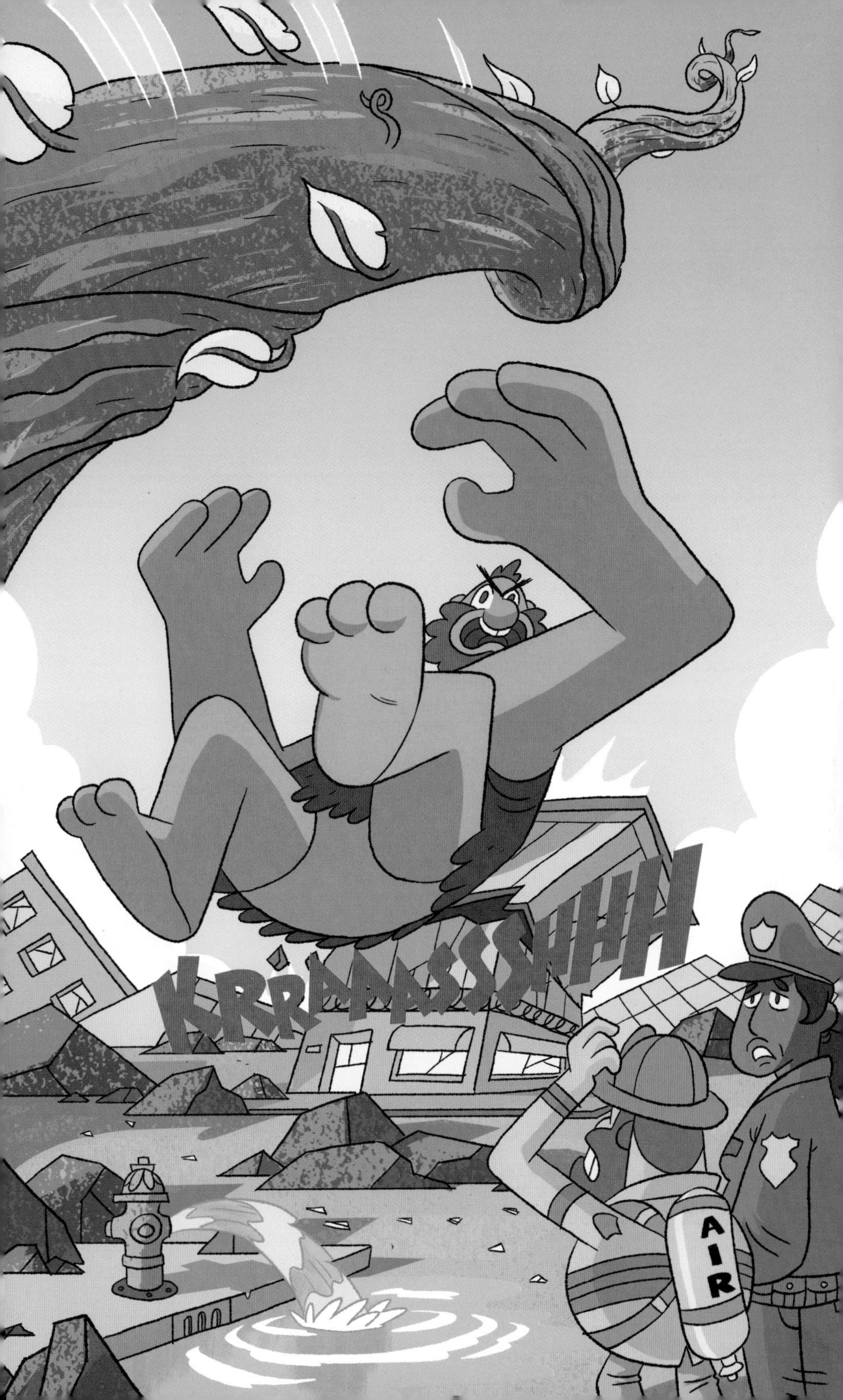
KRRAAASSSHHH
AIR

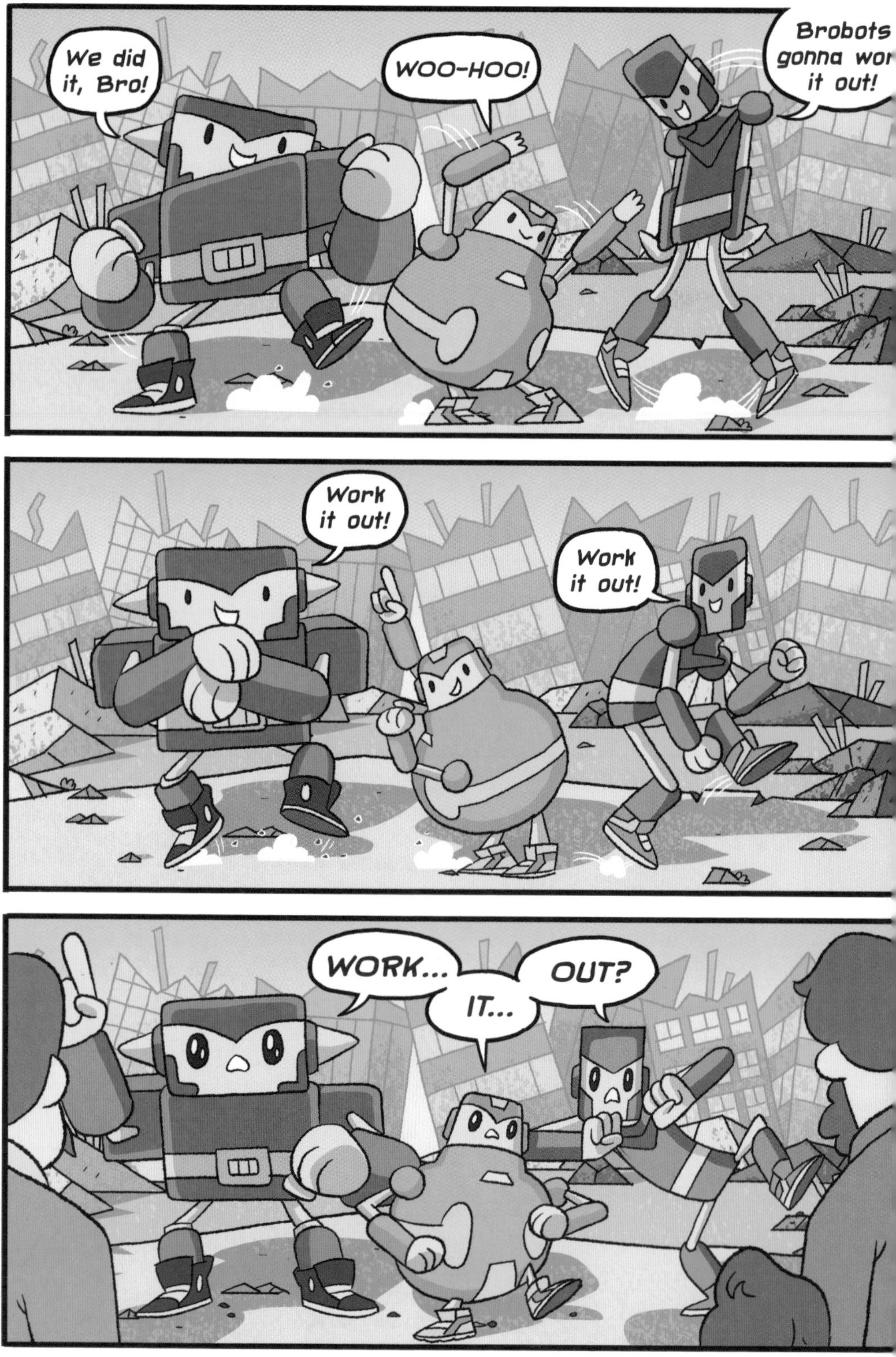
We did it, Bro!
WOO-HOO!
Brobots gonna wor it out!
Work it out!
Work it out!
WORK...
IT...
OUT?

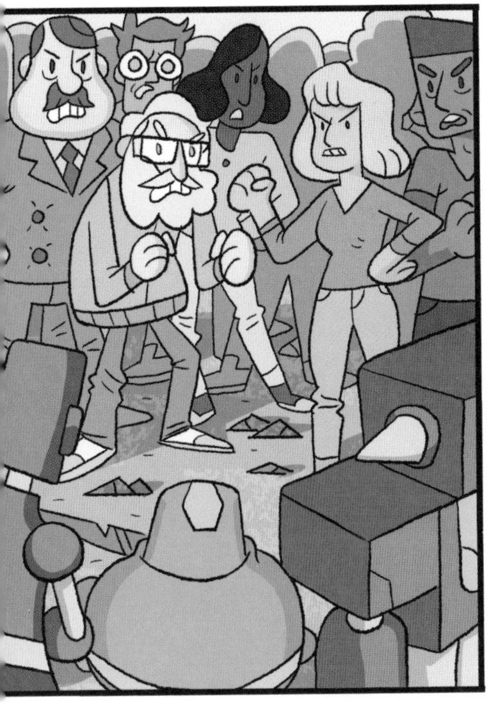

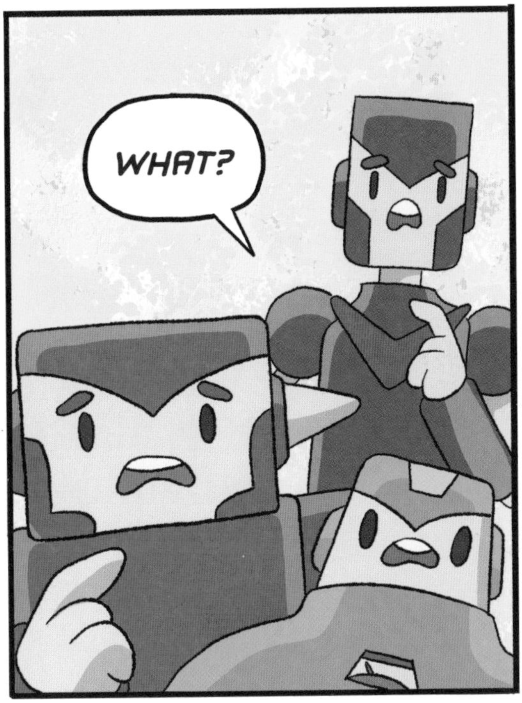
WHAT?

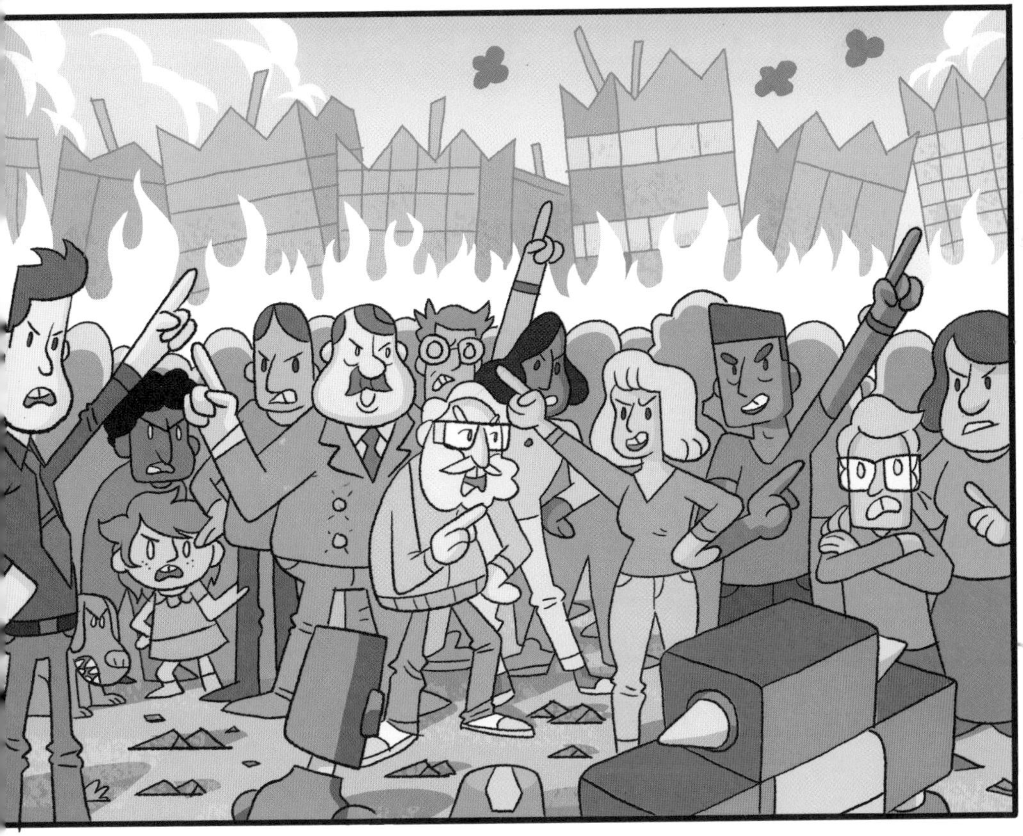

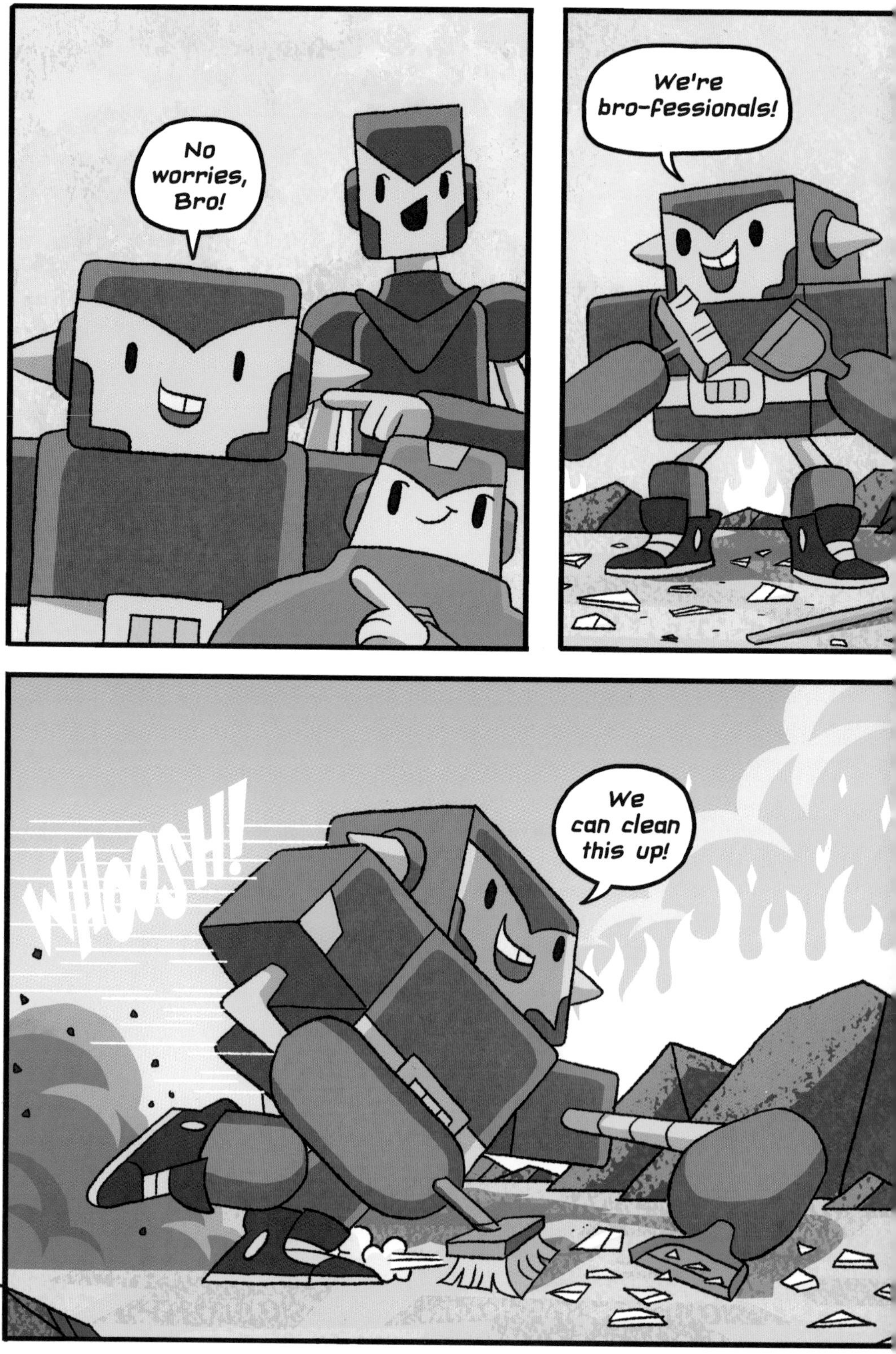
No worries, Bro!
We're bro-fessionals!
WHOOSH!
We can clean this up!

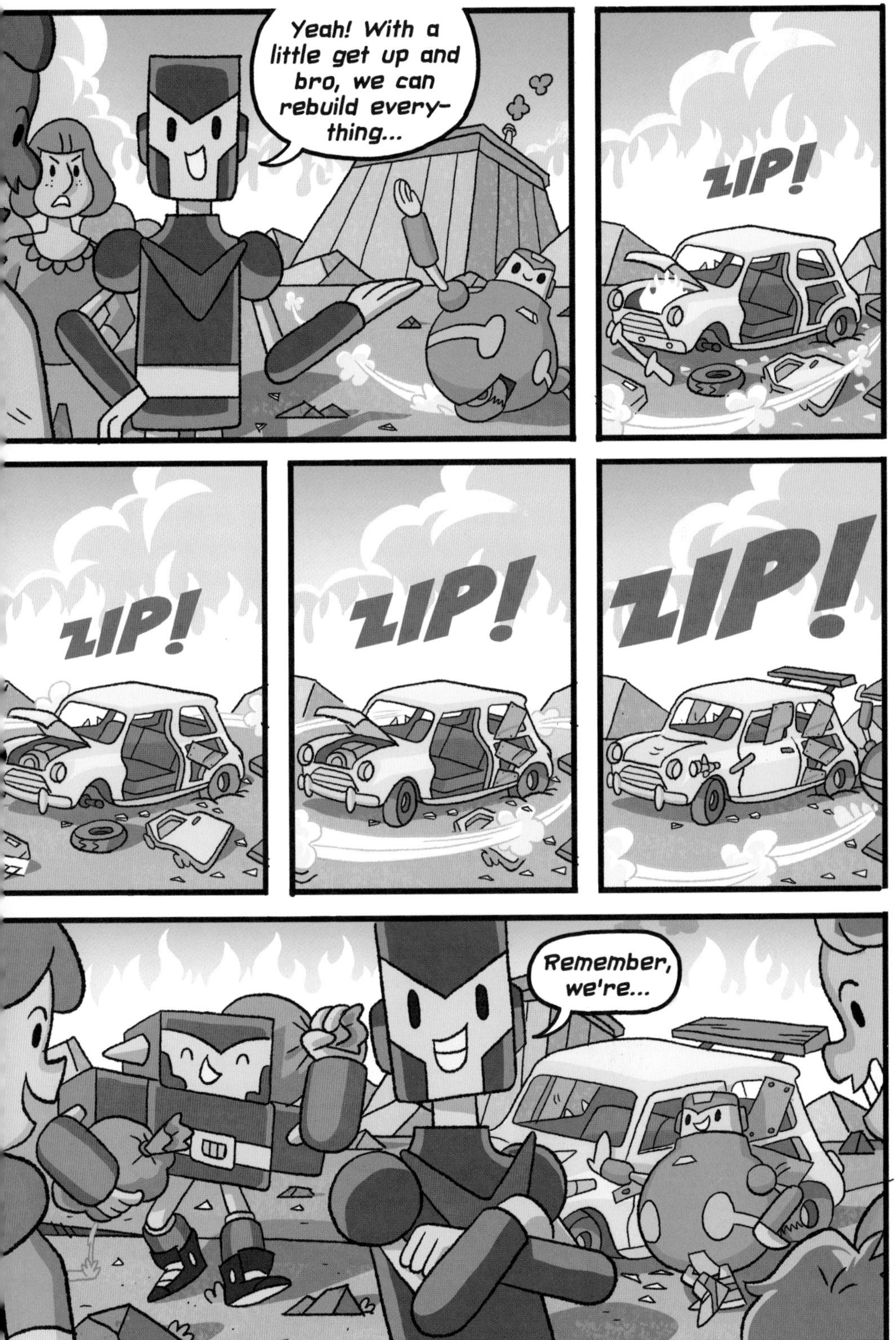
Yeah! With a little get up and bro, we can rebuild every-thing...
ZIP!
ZIP!
ZIP!
ZIP!
Remember, we're...

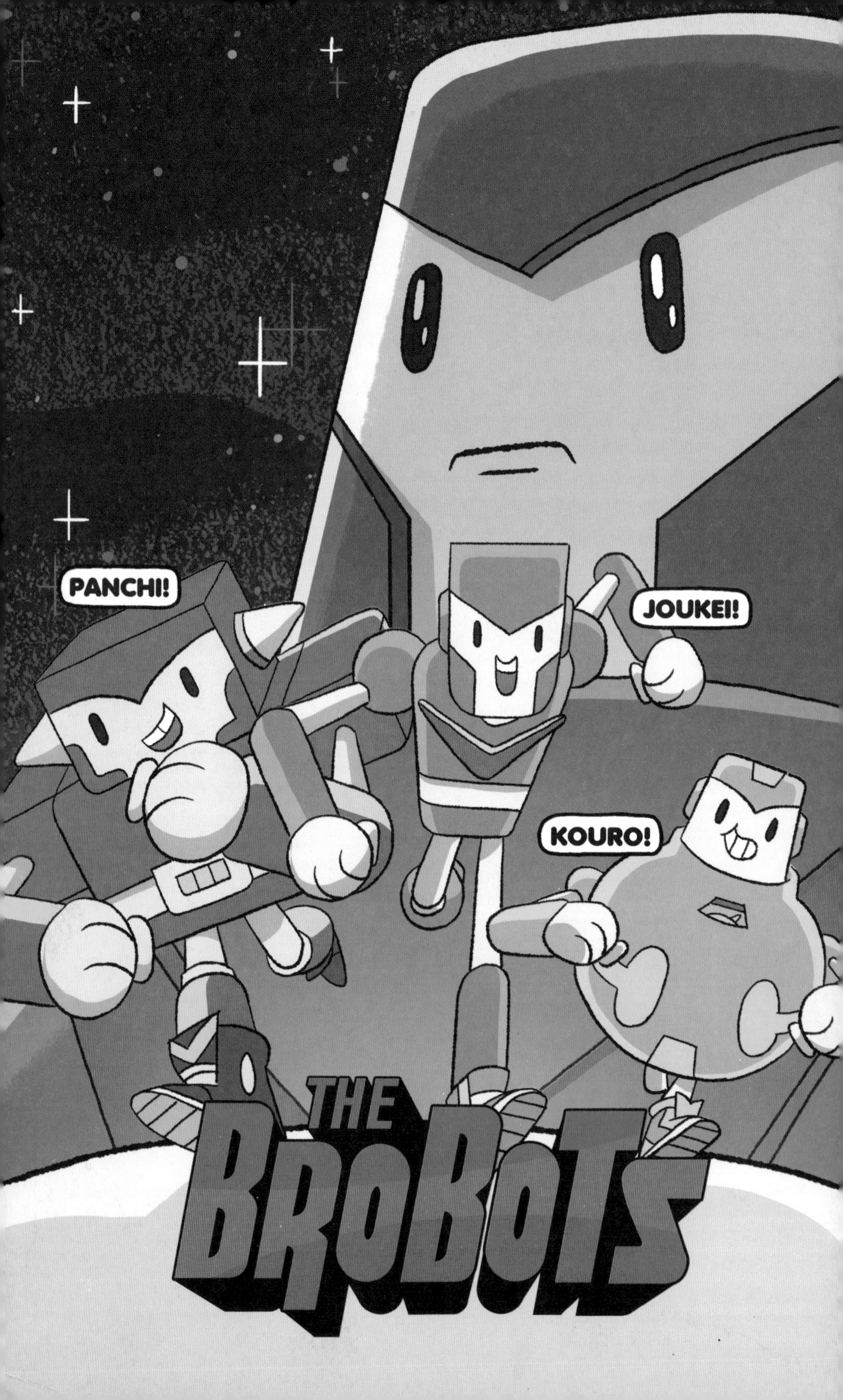
PANCHI!
JOUKEI!
KOURO!
THE BROBOTS

About The Authors

J. TORRES

J. Torres is comic book writer living in Toronto, Canada. His other writing credits include *Alison Dare, Bigfoot Boy, Lola: A Ghost Story, Power Lunch,* and T*een Titans* Go.

His favourite robots are Astro Boy, BB-8, EVE, Giant Robo, and Iron Giant.

J. would like to dedicate this book to his sons Lysandroid 8 and TiBorg IV.

SEAN DOVE

Sean lives and works in Chicago, IL where he runs his one-man design and illustration studio And Thank You For Flying. Sean self-published *The Last Days of Danger*, worked on *Madballs*, and draws his comic series *Fried Rice*.

His favourite robots are Mazinger Z, Astro Boy, TARS, Tetsujin 28, and Gonk.

Sean would like to thank his Parents, Rose and 4 Star Studios.